PLANTATION

PLANTATION

Kervin Giovanni Desir

Photo credits for the topmost photo on the front cover by:
Dr. Dexter J.A. Penn
Tel:+44(0) 744 691 0597
E-mail:dexter.penn@me.com
www.dexterpenn.com

Rev. date: 03/27/2015

To order additional copies of this book, contact:
Xlibris
1-888-795-4274
www.Xlibris.com
Orders@Xlibris.com
642439

CONTENTS

To: Elijah Jaekwon Ali Desir

Nobody's built like you, you design yourself. There is nothing you cannot aspire to and no heights you cannot reach. Son, follow the omens and the universe will conspire in your favour.

-ACT I-

"DREAM DEFERRED"

(THE PLEDGE)

DREAM DEFERRED

What becomes of a dream deferred?
Never to come to fruition
Never seen or heard?
Does it tear the fabric of this sphere; ascend where it rises so high it
becomes unclear?
Or does it disintegrate into the solution of this here?
I promise this isn't natural, these dreams here
These caged in my dome
Unable to breathe the outside air.

Act I – Dream Differed (the pledge)

Interlude

I had to give into the faint trumpet sound that the wind carried, listening now intently, barely hearing the staccato rhythm as it all came to me like a flashing revelation. But it all makes sense. Yes, it does. Intently I roared, enjoying the weight of the truth expelled. But is it all not a casual dance each must play? From the tiniest fabric against the wind's will, to the gravitation of like minds, refining each other through oratory or the germination of a sprout. Such is real, as nature can be simply expressed and yet still be infinitely complex. For the forces at work beneath the surface planted pleasant thoughts, that broke through the soils of disillusionment, blocking my path to the sun. Oh well, is it true that the colour blue stains the brain long after visions fade? So is it true that a single faint trumpet, struggling in frequencies occupied by so much noise, could ring a bell? Any time I revisit her memory I would be temporarily confined to its depths. She, like most others, who seem to wander through my life, had an acute sense of tolerance for the random sparks of genius attributed to my enigmatic antics and the frantic love tales attributed to my curiosity and exploration into love's realm.

CHAPTER 1

Her name is Shari, and she lay still in my dreams, as it seems she had been removed from my reality, my wish was temporary for I never had the chance to say to her what was bleeding out of my eyes every time she stared into mine. Could she tell? As I have been so obvious with my eyes, not only with my bulging bulbs, my body actions would also sell me short. For whenever we hung, it seemed my unawareness of the laws of causality called to me, causality of words and of actions. My foot would somehow enter my mouth without supervision of my brain, that's a feat science can gaze its magnifiers at. How am I to prevent myself from seeming to come off like a complete ass? This answer eludes me presently and if weighted, contributes to already a mountain of complexity that I have no explanation for. Like nature, Shari is unpredictable and therefore dangerous and with this disclaimer I say beware.

Only time will reveal her intentions. Behind that devilish smile an angel sleeps or maybe a freak creeps, terrorizing innocent souls like mine, her voice muffled, passing through like the wind. With her whisper I fell into a trance, the soft trumpet now infecting every part of me, tingling my insides, I'm lost in the unfolding rhythm. She came to me and whispered venom in my ear, sedating my senses, rendering me helpless.

"Hmm…! Don't stop baby, take me there."

I felt her wrapping her warm body around mine, soaking my ear with her venom as I descended deeper. Nothing could paint my feelings as we lay there, she and I. She so soft almost melting with my touch, she tracing my frame as if lost, looking for something, travelling. Her fingers marking her territory as she toyed with me, knowing her destination but lingering, teasing me with the tips of her warm fingers, sending everything inside me mad. Her legs tied around me now, as her lips left my ear, gently wetting my neck, reminding me of all I had been missing, all I had savoured and all that would be mine once again. I heard her giggles and I felt her tug, I heard her moan and saw her smile. All in that single kiss, reconnecting me to that which was far away, but for the moment so near. I love the now and I intend to bask in it for as long as it lasts, her hands inched nearer, closer; as everything is being painted clear – the overdrawn phone calls, making love over the wire, falling asleep; webcams broadcasting rest.

Paralyzed by the thoughts distorted by my ego; the lust. She lay next to me but I can neither trust nor touch her truly. Of course my mind sways in what every direction she lays, what she says awakened a quake which shook, which took away my will to say no. Yes or no, which way should I go? Succumb or overcome. Float or be submerged in the pleasure of her words?

"Almost there, baby." She nibbled on my ear, her hands pasting now, leaving behind warmth as it left my upper body, grabbing my manhood. It all ended in a flash as my annoying phone alarm sent displeasure through me.

"Ahhhhhhhhh, Nooooooo!"

I wish I could remain dreaming, just dreaming, forever living in these times that cushion my existence and keep me sane. Desperately fighting the urge to awaken from this slumber, my phone alarm now escalates to new heights, sending a streak of irritation through my head. Sometimes I feel like throwing you against the wall and dismembering you, leaving you severed, dislocating your keypad from your microphone, sending my SIM ascending high and hoping it does fall victim to gravity. Wasted thought, as I am brought back to reality and reminded of its cost.

Of course, now I know why I wrestle from sleep every morning, could it be that my 'tracking device' or as they call it, "blackberry", reminds me constantly of its cost? And the cost of maintaining a status that would have me wearing you on my belt on that daily as an emblem of my affordability—of such a nuisance of technology. But wait, there has to be more to all of this, I thought, as I proceed to drag myself to the kitchen. It was no use going in there, for the fridge was bare and opening it would remind me of its nakedness as I drank from the kitchen faucet, although there was cold water in there. But I couldn't bear the coldness of the water so early, for I soon had to battle with the ever colder reality that awaits me outside.

Damn, I overslept again. What if you had been alarmed but were never aware of the impending danger approaching as you walked through life? What is it with alarms anyway that sends impulses to the brain, that forces action or reflex and gets the body mobile again? To think that we would rather labour, than to make our fantasies wander, all this entertained me as I began my routine. That thought woke me as I went back in my room, reached to turn the alarm off and sighed after realizing that I'd had lost the beauty in the imagery unfolding a few seconds ago. That of my dream, of course, these are like movies for resting souls, which console and expose all thos,e fantasies that roam in the subconscious. The water from the shower has a crude way of reminding you of how cold the temperature is as it hit my face, killing every ounce of sleep I had left.

CHAPTER 2

Please excuse me for my brash delivery and tactless introduction, but my name is …….. ah forget it, it doesn't even matter how I am labeled, for I am still unable to permit the slightest inquiry into my life's mystery. I have always felt a shadow of loneliness behind me, accompanying me. Altogether I have become quite used to its darkness, for who knows you better than your shadow— well, except God, of course— and who would foster the destruction of that which gives it shape, gives it life, for without me it would cease to be apparent? And therefore for the duration of this rendition I will remain nameless and assume the mystique of a shadow. I am but a boy in this world of men, in this world of sin, I experience through these optics as I struggle with my identity like the shadow, my destiny, my place in this god forsaken place. I am like you; often curious with no real leads in my quest, only an ideal encompassing all that I know, all that I wish to know and all that carries in the desires of my dreams. Until now I have realized the gravity of this dilemma which I wish to share with you. 'Tis a tale we can all relate to. I find myself eager to do or to create something, anything that will distinguish me from this labyrinth of nonsense I come into contact with daily. My characteristics are that of an eccentric, often misunderstood by others. The labels are many, some say outcast, some say rebel, some even say I possess the acute sense of expression resembling that of an insane asylum patient. That's another problem, I have the tendency to embellish how I am perceived and so I become my own worst enemy when I paint these.

When I create, it is the only time I truly feel free without bounds. The water drops on the hibiscus leaves, trickles down to the ground, quenching the morning soil, as the morning news always seems to waken everything, especially the controversies of the times—The political landscape, the playground for men, debating on how much spent, stories of tragedy and tales of triumph. The static from the distorted frequencies coats the broadcast with an authenticity, it's hard to describe but it makes it sound all the more now, relevant to the times we are living and reminiscent of the static around us. Static brought about by collisions. Collision of egos, of greed; man's preoccupation with amassing what is foremost, not even his to begin with. Frolicking in the desperate pits of despair and contempt, the masks they wear to conceal their conscious identities are the very frequencies we tune into on the daily. Leaving us to listen only to their voices, not knowing who's a genuine oracle or who's some propagandist stirring up mischief.

Speaking now in descriptive diction the announcer shares a series of facts, breaking my concentration, dangling on the high-wire, losing balance, falling into its depth like Dante in *This inferno* as I for a brief moment sympathize with all the casualties—that is, until other news comes blowing by. The flood of information makes it harder to embrace anything. I constantly find myself juggling tasks, multitasking without asking. What's the point of all this flood of information anyway? A young woman in her early twenties, barely getting-by, is unaware of her pending assault, the assailant giving a horror of a show as he slashes her, like she was mere flesh; she is surprised by the cutlass greeting from her boyfriend that leaves her disfigured permanently. All is reverent; cannot love or even lust justify the actions of men? And so what now possesses them? Is it that the world's primitive cold nature is somehow perspiring through the paws of man, clouding our better judgement? Or is the mind an unkempt garden, growing wild, weeds chaotic in their sprung, and with no higher deity to plough? The garden that will always grow is the mind, as you all know, learning is not only literal in perception but sensual in affection, the embrace of the moment gives it relevance.

Now the sports announcer quotes stats on everyone, from the cricket player to the foreign football quarterback who ran almost two times over the perimeter of the field in one game. I myself always rather lend my ear to the discussion and calling sessions- "What makes me mad."

Caller: "Hello"

Announcer: "Yes, good day caller, you are on the air. Now tell us what makes you mad".

Caller: "The water, the pressure is too high, the pressure is so high in the Dennery area that the pressure already bust my pipe. And I just wanted to tell the authorities of Wasco to ease on de pressure."

Announcer: "Is that all caller?"

Caller: "Yes, oh, and de government bringing pressure too."

The exchanges amuse me at times, for their contributions are sometimes elaborate attempts at saying, "Hey, look at me, I can speak!" - hardly speaking most of the time and simply running around playing games, toying with the audience's ear. The mission is accomplished, don't blame the medium; it is just the recipient of the product that man produces extending his influence to the audience aboard the morning bus.

CHAPTER 3

I contribute to arguably one of the greatest schemes man has ever designed. A number of mutual, stocks, bonds and co-operations form its skeleton. I work for the assurance industry, where I occupy the post of one who ensures that the computerized machinery behaves in accordance with the users' desires. Printing, scanning, backing up, filing, modifying, commuting; all over copper wires hidden under ceiling tiles on top of me. All these cables running all over the building and all assembling in this refrigerated office called the IT department.

The building was a conventional office building, like those of most businesses which deal in selling insurance. Before its concrete structure stretches a car park able to park 50 vehicles with ease. Approaching the building you would inevitably be taken by the always perfectly trimmed hedges and lawns prize cut, always sporting that fresh-from-the-barber look, decorated with elaborate yellow daffodil patches, strategically planted along the clay brick footpath leading to the tinted double glass door marking its entrance. Whoever birthed the ideas of selling people peace of mind shares the same mechanics as all those **con**fident men who pride themselves on amassing what someone else owns by means of (as I call it) linguistic swindling and cunning legislation.

Insurance is an asset and yes everything to me seems to revolve around this capitalist concept. For, acts of man or God may place an unfortunate burden on the unsuspecting hence, car insurance, home insurance, life insurance: all these insure peace of mind to the customers who willingly pay handsomely for coverage in the event shit happens. In case shit happens to your car, you know you will be covered for the damages, say in the event your transport gets turned into scrap metal. Or in case hurricane winds send the roof of your house toppling.

My, my! Every time I enter the building, everything seems so settled and positioned so perfectly. From the founding partners group picture overlooking a mantelpiece leaning against the wall next to the stairway adding sparkles of silver and gold trophies amassed by the apparently successful organization, to all the other discreet fittings that make for a corporate outfit. I am usually late, by this time 8:57 telephones singing was already apparent, the beeping of the fax machine, the spitting of the copier, the remnants of polite morning conversation, all in tune to the beat of covered feet against rubber tiles. Tack tack, tack tack, high heels, low heels, heelless all tapping, drumming to this musical. Now upstairs, maneuvering through the maze of cubicles to the blue door written: Information System Department. Rushing now to my blue haven, greeting persons stationed along the highway as I make my way to my station before someone high up the hierarchy spots me walking in with my workbag swinging over my shoulder. Before I knew it I turn the knob and enter, quickly shutting the door behind me.

Seconds later my phone rang, it was my father and he wants to see me. Damn, I can't believe this man. Already! Knocking down the wall in front of me would be a more worthy task for me now, tensing muscles wanting to hit something, anything that would render me numb temporarily while I take in everything the boss had to say. I hadn't even let go of my bag and already…sigh.

Walking casually along the corridor, thinking of a story to explore… I'm tired of fiction anyway. I'll just tell him I overslept on account of my phone going dead so it didn't alarm. Slam! A story in under 20 seconds and to think you can add a little sprinkle of reality to your fiction and make it come to life. It sounds believable, it has become a habit of mine of late, that is, waking up late. I swear the nights are something else these days. I can't get any sleep for the life of me. I think it's beginning to affect my nerves. I really need some rest from this. Apart from those elaborate dreams of Shari and a few laughs with the boys, I haven't been living to my fullest. There's this void that's growing. I can sense it. Is love here? It's just a joy for me seeing granny still here. I'm glad she's alive and healthy. I think she scared death away with her courage.

CHAPTER 4

The life is one hell of a ride where your destination might be right over the curb. The life's preparation for death made for a great thriller or a drama, littered with action or rattled with insult. At this time I find it hard to embrace every magnetic impulse that has me attached to this place. Me, fearing death's grasp has caused me to hide behind the rail guards of life while pedestrians prance in their Sunday best concealing all the anguish with adventure, as their alcohol sips draw them close to this hypnotic state where all notions are lost and the now is left to prevail. I want the now again or something that stimulates me, anything but this. I dread this place. It's a fact that has been slowly coming to light as of recent and I can't bear to figure out why.

Sorry story anyway, I pity the fool who buys it. I was just a little late that's all. You don't complain when I work late with no overtime pay anyway, so why should you when I come in a little late? Lost in the commotion in my mind, ignoring everyone as I passed the cubicle lineup. Then this accounts clerk grinned at me like something's funny. Early morning out your life— assuming a post for the day while you pray for it to be over - just to give you enough time to rest for the next. And you smile! I smiled back, remembering her from something a while back. Hell, you can't even rest, I'm lucky I don't have any responsibilities, no obligations, diapers or none of that. I'm just here to work and to run shit. I was indoctrinated and fed western education till I thought I was smart because I understood how ones and zeros were manipulated on a computer. Damn, they can fool you.

I can't get this feeling, out ahhhhh!
Like an itch you can't reach
Bothering me, to the point of insanity.
Thinking 'bout me, my life, that sad state it has been reduced to.
Squeeze me like lime, make juice with my head, I feed on all y'all garbage anyway.
Can't stand seeing cans with picture of treats, like meats, but is it really?
Toy with your boy, trick me, turn me over like an old mattress or even worse, like an old politician.
Can't stand up..............Can't stand this feeling.
Yesterday I went to church, Friday I attended Jumu'ah at the mosque.
I still feel something, something dark and true
Parading, around imitating us, disguised as us, wondering everywhere on every label at every store.

I'm sure you've seen it. Sometimes she smiles but you know what's underneath that smile,
Her teeth's always out, ready to bite! Really? I could be silly but I'm real! And you know it.
Standing around waiting to just smile at everything and all the while there ain't nothing to smile about.
I seen something!
I always wondered what it was. Can't name it but its resemblance is prevalent out there.
Space out there, but inside here is even more space. I feel empty and hollow.
And more conflict and more love, more food and more people. More people out here walking around like ain't nothing wrong with that. Ain't nothing wrong with us.
Being empty!
I seen something aright! Something that cause you to crawl in doubt - stick your tale between your legs. Boy!
That's right.
Something so wrong for so long it became right. Like black folk all of a sudden turning white. Ain't none of my business but I seen it, I bet you seen it too.
Thinking rent's due.........
What you call writin', I call clearin' my mind.
Yesterday I was stressin', rent's due.
Last night ended up in a gentleman's club, front row view.
Found myself lost in her crotch, thinkin' how many negroes been through.

Still hung a bill snug along her laces tapped her gluteus, drinkin Moet out the bottle, quenchin' demons…

You might as well been too!
Then when you see it you say: to each his own.
I seen a dog, patched up, limping, the bitch looked like she just lost a fight. A car slowed down, a frail hand flung a bone across the street. The dog didn't even flinch; it looked away like some'em wrong with you.
Can't even decide if my eyes seen true, it was late and I had already drowned myself.
Feeling like a fish.
Thinking about being frustrated and broke and everything. Lost in debt not even 25 yet.
Can even tell what's genuine from fake, I take it all in with a sprinkle of sin. It's inevitable, right?

This morning I came to work and this place for a split second resembled…I don't even wanna say it, besides we's modern now, aint't it?
I could hear the machines taunting me as I come in.
Hiding behind doors of smile, too addicted to rituals….too dead to live.

Wake up your daughter!
Tell her get ready for her shift.
Tell her how she overslept again.
Or lack thereof rest.
Can she appreciate toiling all night?
To awake dissatisfied just to repeat last night,
Is it something to smile about?
I doubt!
Moving on to better times where you created and communicated between these halls.
If these halls could speak.
If these cash draws could replicate the amount.
I assure you they can't.
Cause it would speak of lost souls like yours.
Lost souls, who saw being behind this desk as a stepping stone.
Ended up chained to that stone.
Running around my mind, ever distancing from the only thing I knew
After being bred a "thoroughbred"
Plump on western ideology.
'Get a number and fall in the race.'

That's what the man said. I looked at his face and saw tracks running across his forehead, tobacco weathered teeth and that same ole crooked smile. All the while. In a blink, his face turned to mine—
I know what to do!

With that last theatrical act playing out in my mind, I approached his office door, hurrying in – as if in a hurry.

CHAPTER 5

"How many times I told you to knock before you enter?" he said, in a harsh tone.

"Plenty", I said to myself, in my throat.
"Sorry, daddy…I mean, boss."

He said my name then proceeded. "What is it that you have with rules, anyway?"

Before I could answer he went on in a more serious tone, one that I had expected. He continued rattling.

My eyes travelled around his office, to anything but him. I couldn't bear to look him. I couldn't bear look him in the eye, couldn't bear to stare. Something happened to us. There was no longer love there, no, we only tolerated each other and had grown to be entire opposites. Should I have expected different? I was never drawn to the life he subscribes to, well, partially. I'd understood the reasons for upwards mobility but until now I never thought it would be this demanding on my faculties. Also I never anticipated it would be such a bore: one lame monotone hump that required cutthroat antics the higher you got.

He continued on, hardly keeping up, lost in his office surroundings. What does he know anyway? I can't expect him to understand my predicament, we are from two different worlds; me living on the fringes, exposed to the cold 'mongst folks with few options, him living adventurous, awning shades shelters, far removed from persistent sirens.

"You got that!"

"Yes daddy, sorry; yes boss!"

He went on for about 5 minutes, all that time my tummy playing an organized solo. I was so hungry. Can't even remember when we last had a conversation. I've gotten used to him speaking at me, so much so I was certain we couldn't. Maybe he saw something in me that resembled my mother's free spirit and that probably may have turned him off.

Thinking of the last time I can remember him carrying me, distracted slightly by this folding memory creeping that seems to arise and soothe my stomach's moans as if interested in the feeling it arose.

What inspires the MC to captivate the crowd before him? Is he seen through their eyes as a mere entertainer or is he something more, quenching the dry dullness of the times and making it wet with excitement? His aura draws numbers, who flock like obedient sheep, in unison; all in motion to one beat as his voice rattles without retreat into the airways, flocking the circumference as the sound plays melodies drowning all. The air was thick with the odor of perspiration as the crowd towered over me. All I could see was masses above me, yellow shirts hung from the trees and people singing to a chant, 'U.W.P! We party!' Trying to make sense of the conjoined expression, my head started to hurt. I felt a beating in my head like an annoying sync which ran like a pulse knocking down all sense inside my head. Tagged along still as I felt his hand would slip and I would be permanently lost in this sea of yellow shirts. It lasted for about half an hour then suddenly the crowd was parted by a white SUV with stickers all over it bearing the picture of a man's face with "Vote Yellow" written across. Standing through the sun roof, a man with a wide brim straw cowboy hat spoke slowly into a megaphone:
"Make way, make way I say
Today I say make way
For a new regime today
Enough play, it's time we take way Lucia from this nightmare!"

I could barely make out what was said as the crowd's roar covered his delivery, as the SUV steadily made its way towards the stage. Civilized folk turning hostile, jumping and screaming, as the SUV passes by like some hall of fame rock star happens to be inside. Up until now I had never seen such a sight, well, except on TV, but the realness of it mixed with the chaos and the noise and all the energy being dispersed, all made it so magical. I'm sure I would become detached or even worse, my father would lose his grip of my hand and I would be forever lost in what was becoming a rough sea. I tugged at his yellow shirt and held out both my hands up, giving him a sign to put me on his shoulder.

The stage seemed hugely decorated with faces of men who looked familiar, although I had never seen or known any, they just seemed to have that familiar face, you know, that politician enchanting stare, even apparent in my tyke days. But how had I sensed that even as a mere boy was beyond me. Although I didn't have the ability to articulate these thoughts, there was something in me, something from my little experience. I had grown all too familiar with this stare. About twelve of them, men pictured all in a line. As my eyes traced the line of the portraits, I realized I was wrong, for there was one face which bore the signature of sincerity. I examined his face and tried to make sense out of this orange in a lemon pile.

T-shirts were being flung haphazardly from the stage as the SUV now made its way to the back. Now everyone was in yellow, I mean everyone — even the vendors, the cameramen, the children, the wives, the mothers. I think the police on the bikes were jealous and wanted to join the carnival as they stared seriously from the sidelines. The MC now started to speak, giving a brief introduction as he proceeds to introduce who I believe was the man of the hour.

"He's been there before and he has proven to be for the people, he's been away from the arena for a while but I know he's still for the people. My people, allow me to welcome on the stage, Sir John Compton!"

I was shocked as speakers from the sidelines blasted a song introducing a giant. The yellow hairs on my arms stood in reverence as he graced the stage with an elegance that would mistake him for a king. I wasn't taught how to feel how I felt that day as I watched that man walk on stage; each stride taking him closer and I further from where my childhood thoughts could reach. I had heard over the radio of Sir John, and in school, although I hadn't really paid attention, when my teacher spoke about him in social studies. How can one man possess so much power with just his stride? I wouldn't subside. This curiosity was consuming me as the ground literally shook as he made his way to the mic. Seconds were stretched to infinity, it seemed to me, and I now dying with anticipation to hear and see what this whole thing was all about. Why was I feeling this way? Why was the crowd also in sync with my feeling? Why did my dad came to this thing? I sensed as if strands of history were accumulating here and this event had some profound and important role in our island— laughing to myself, I thought, gone are the days my mind would be so young, naïve, and impressionable.

I suddenly felt a drop and then some more as rain made its entrance, obviously not wanting us to witness this historic event. My father rushed me out of the crowd as the rain got heavier, manoeuvering through the sea of wet yellow; no one seemed to move, unflinching as they stood in the downpour. He held me in both my arms, lifted me and held me tight, sheltering my head from the downpour. The sound now disappeared as we moved further and the rain took over. What was it in that moment which made it possible for so much energy to be conducted into this communal? I thought… being carried always felt better, especially in the rain, for some reason. But he must have had something magical for all these people to be moved. Our people are hell to move and he did it with just a stride, far more if I had heard the address.

"So, I expect you know all your antics have been tolerated long enough, it's time you settle down in your new post and embrace your new responsibilities like a responsible young man."

"Is that it?" I said in a hungry tone. Mumbling, "Added responsibilities without added pay." I stood up …was about to speak, then someone opened the door and entered. She paid no mind intruding on our informal meeting, interrupting my chain of thought. I would have stated my frustrations before the door knob turned and now I was blank, walking out the office unnoticed as she went on, closing the door behind me.

CHAPTER 6

A coalition of personalities, assembled in between these halls daily. An ensemble deliberately placed there on the scene, commuting through highways with no reflectors and streets with no lights. As I walk to my station, I have gotten used to them and considered them all members of an unwanted extended family I have grown quite fond of. Although I sensed pity in me, for some reason, I never could address this. I often dismissed it thinking that there was nothing to feel pity for. I almost never had an honest free sprinting conversation with anyone there, for it seemed like there was always something wrong when I opened my mouth, on account that when I spoke assertively of topics and things far from their narrow perspectives I would be often misinterpreted as just being brash and condescending. But I loved everyone anyway. I have grown quite used to being misunderstood and for this very reason I keep a tightly knit circle. You have the mango of my eyes, Shari of course. Although she was far away at present we still shared everything and every experience. When I'm not conspiring over the wire with her, I was raising all kinds of hell with the boys: the trio, Danny, Simon and I were inseparable and hung so much that we resembled each other. Well, up until lately, for I haven't had much free time at my disposal.

These are the happiest days of my life, despite this feeling creeping. I enjoy the collage of people around me, especially at work, colouring my life in grey scales and dull shades. Some yellow, some red and some green with envy. Then you have the yes men, the grapevine-ers, the house Negroes, the field Negroes, the lazy, the confrontational, the complacent, the diligent and some with a combination of these tendencies and some coming to work to get a life; to meddle in others' lives, that is. And not forgetting those who come simply to pass the time, hoping to be compensated adequately for time traded. I often marvel at the picture unfolding before my frames,

21

for it seems like I was constantly questioning it. It felt like it was all a déjà vu, a repeat of something history spoke. History's chewing gum that had lost all taste. Every day I pace these halls and every day the same shit, different scenarios though, but the same shit none the less. As far as being a responsible corporate citizen, the company played its part at masquerading – having their marketing ploys appear humanitarian. And the public just eats it all up, no salt, the filthier the better.

Of late my mind has been bending still, bending in every direction of the light. I need an insurrection; I need a resurrection, a revolution, any oddity or climate that's conducive to helping me reach my peak. My current low is as a result of me not envisioning the plateau, or me lacking the ability to attract my ideal situation, as I feel like my woes are constantly being boomeranged. I walked back to my desk and got back to the ritual.

-ACT II-

"Delusions of Grandeur"

(The Turn)

Delusions of grandeur

How can we be saved, most of our young soldiers are preoccupied on getting high on life, the rest are puppets behind some desk somewhere or chasing some feeble ideal, busy pushing buttons in a box.
Mind you they grow up to be as trained - Nothing more.

Voices from the under whisper tales in the wind
Not for sale! Not for sale!
Oil makes rainbows in the drain
Child dies, many cry, seen so much promise in his eyes.
Men die, chasing canvases in the sky
No one cries eyes too still to pry.

The clock isn't deterred by perils
Every *tic* is a genesis,
Every *toc* in a feeble apocalypse.
Lost so much sleep to dreams, so it seems
Choice is eventful, not to be deliberated with thought.
Mine's the battle of the ages, I'm caught
Matter not what become
All that matters is-
one more soul added to sorrows told.

Act II – Delusions of grandeur (*the turn*)

Interlude

Each wave is identical in its elegance, the identical process forms them all and they all beat the surface of the shores. So what makes one wave stand out? What makes it transcend time?

A wave of great magnitude carrying disaster like that of a tsunami may cast a shadow about the millions which brush the shores. It becomes eternal, only in its destructive nature does it become permanent in the minds of men. For it would live in infamy, forever in history through articles, through elaborate stories passed down to showcase its destructive beauty. And through art; on the surface it may be represented by a painter's vivid recollection of the waves' graphic or through the literature left from the narrator's story. All these are mere essentials to the wave's life and with each stroke a different dimension is added to something that lasted a mere minute.

"All is not lost", said the preacher to the family whose sea side shack was reduced to rubble. "For the actions of God, however crude", he continued, "they may seem, have an underlining."

Pardon my questioning the will of God but what is the underlining when all she had, the little her earning could purchase, the priceless memories of her two little children playing in their 2 by 4 world, what could she have possibly done to deserve such a fate? Some things lost may never be regained and it may be useless spending our lives searching through the rubble and debris trying to recover past memories.

Love is inexhaustible and therefore the root of love must not be subjected to question rather be embraced however bitter the taste. 'Cause God is love and love not only heals all past wounds, it also scars its victims while soothing the soul. It is the weapon which heals.

Each life is a blink in the time's eyes.
Man is an infant, on accord he can't outlive the trees, rocks, peaks, stationary voiceless figures; figures stationary in their majesty, forgotten portraits of divinity, mammoths in man's brash accomplishments.

Embrace the infinite and stretch to transcend. Only nature's touch creates true masterpieces void of the signature of man. Only through primitive lenses man makes his true masterpiece. We are still children excavating dirt; don't let conformity be part of your vocabulary.

CHAPTER 7

Good afternoon, Lucia, I am awake! It's me again. Eager to depart from my ritual as I ride from this place, this tomb, no... this temporary cold storage; and I raise from my slumber. It's 4:30 pm to be accurate, 4:29:59, to be precise. This is when I clock out and my mind clocks out to the regular as I linger in the city for a while.

The block presently known as X, marks the central station where we would location, lime, loft, whatever you wanna call it and talk until sun doze, then some more. Ladies, girls, women, duffle bags, backpacks and pulses decorate the streets on this lime. Friday is the end of shitty week and the eve of the weekend, which you rather spend sipping some brew with crew or sticking some dime that blew. Anyhow this was a rare occasion when I decided to actually loft on the block. I usually pass the block while en route, making hand gestures to my peers, jamming while scanning the scene, looking for new hens. I had to meet Simon, there. I hadn't seen him for a week now and he kept texting me about this scene he had to put me on, not knowing what, but his insistence seemed to signify something really important. He wouldn't disclose any detail but insisted we link. I was eager, been wanting to jump on that scene from a week ago, whatever it is, but I been so busy I didn't get the chance to pursue what he had. Could it be the same grin he was telling me about a couple months ago? Choops, I hope not. These days I seem to have little tolerance for these girls and their games. I have to stay focused, stay faithful. Faithful to what, I said to myself, while I entertained partners I hadn't seen in a while. Looking at my watch every few minutes as my wait was prolonged for an hour, much longer than I had expected. It's not like I had anything to do at the moment, so what the hell, I didn't mind the wait, and it gave me time to catch up on things. I was approached by this girl who took all time away anyway.

It has been three months since I have gone out, three months since I last took a woman's scent. I had learnt to savour the all too familiar one which lingered in my mind, the last real memory I could find. I have learnt to forget everything which kept me in the rat race. I was dazzled by her curves as she spoke, but unenthusiastically going along. I bumped into an old friend in town and we spoke for a while, well she spoke of old times but they seemed foreign to me. Anyway, she invited me out to this house party vibe her cousins would be having and without the hint of hesitation I played along, accepting her invitation. Her name sounded familiar— Keisha, but that was just about it for her, I didn't really care, for Shari's scent still lingered in the mind's hallway; all day.

Maybe, just maybe, Shari's memory won't die and she won't cease to exist in time and our once cherished thoughts would be retraced by a more sober moment where logic would be the principle by which I abide and the now would be less refined and more fluid. I would be at work and she at school and we would cease to exist and simultaneously be somewhere that our thoughts or our touch could grasp. Elaborate hues of grey exchanged for a more rational feel, one without love's stain, as I refrain from mentioning her name.

At last he came and told me we have to link up tonight. Danny wants us to link up tonight up north.
"What you up to?"

"Nothing," I said hastily as I quickly discarded that thing, that last thought that I had harboured.
"So you on the low dem days, boy," he said inquisitively. "Mun say you have *go pwell!*" (*a local term currently used to describe symptoms of lovelorn*), he said laughingly.

I just looked back and smiled, simply glad that I was acknowledged again by someone within my circle, one of the few people who really had my back.

"What you doin' now, dog? I go check you up north, I going home to eat, rest and to get ready for later. Later, doggy."

He jammed me and we went our separate ways, me to my bus stand ééhe to his.

CHAPTER 8

"Yow!" a voice from behind me yelled.

Now seeing this man extending his begging hand towards me.

"Wha you want?" I returned.
"Move from dere."
"Vyé zombi" (old jumbie)
"Soti" (move from there)
I gave a firm stare but I felt low, trying not to succumb to my crippling emotions. I have a soft spot for these guys. I didn't even have change to spare.

"Wait, Sir, is something I have to ask you."

Returning his stare as he spoke he broke through the glare.

"Imagine I here for nine thousand years now, you see that."
He pointed across the road. I couldn't help but stare and stray away from whatever it was which shaped my day in such an unpleasant way. I became at once fixated on this two-wheel trolley. Tireless, rims bare, standing upright with an ole sugar sack with whatever was inside, held to the trolley by what appeared to be rope of some sort, the kind they use to tie those sacks. Running endlessly round and round the trolley, those old cords, them so old they broke in strands like floss. The trolley, coloured with paint from top to bottom: red paint, white paint, yellow paint and random drops of green paint. No doubt, an attempt to disguise its rusting surface. It stood about 5 feet from the ground balanced by the wheels of steel holding to the sack, looking forced to carry the load. Tangled and knotted and roped.

I looked around, few people in sight. I saw a coconut vendor talking and people blazing by, trying to keep up with the race as they hasten past without the slightest inquiry. A little after 5pm now as the atmosphere in town resembled that of a Sunday afternoon. The air was dead and so was the Ville: persons commuting, but it still dead. The sun seemed to have the father's fury, unforgiving, baking everything except the mad man, my face drenched salty as I tried to remember what de ass I was upset about now, folding my sleeves, exposing my roots to the sun.

I scanned the top and turned to him and said, "Why you have dem two flags sticking out the two handles?" clearly forgetting I was upset and en route.

Without answering, he smiled.
"You see that there, that's mi baby, any time I mad I go get she. I couldn't help seeing you from there", he said. "It's just that I ain't used to seeing you, especially on the block, it don't look like you," he said in a rush. "All dressed up with your tie and all, you looking out of place."

I didn't even answer. It was a long day and all my mind was bent on now was later. I know them fellas and I know how they roll, playing superstar ting when out in public, especially under the influence. And Friday night presents any excuse to celebrate, mingling and vibes. The thing I find rather interesting of late is that they regularly complain about being broke but they manage to go out more.

He continued, "It look like you ain't had a bean in you all day. Look there bouy, young strapping man how you looking so? I seen you by the block a while ago and say to myself, da'mun looking funny dere. I became even more curious as I realized dem feelings your face held."

I suddenly realized I hadn't eaten. My mind was racing so much and at the back of it all, I didn't have a good day at work today, thank God it's Friday. Although it's Friday, I still felt a tad down, still down, still quizzed with this feeling. I didn't even realize this feeling had been reflected on my visage all this time. Showing through my facial all this time? I mean all day! I tried to look through the storefront but I swear I couldn't see my face. All I saw was the reflection of people pacing and this figure before me. But how could he tell?

"You see my trolley here?" he continued, still pointing.

"I come with the most wholesome, most local, most tasty, most reasonable cassava bread in the city."

He went on rhyming out of timing and performing more and selling less. I continued to listen.

"Mostly specialize in cassava but due to customer request I making sea moss, de most potent moss anywhere in de ville. Don't let me start.... You ain't look like you will need any sea moss today," he said, seeming to prick me to amuse him.

After trying to sell me cassava bread and realizing I wasn't lying when I told him I didn't have any money apart from transport fee on hand he decided to give me one, insisting I take it. I told him I would pay him on my next visit to the city, as the sun slowly made its exit. His offering seemed like a gesture inviting me to hear him out as he went on talking.

"What's your name?"

I didn't answer. I returned with the same question. Then he went on.

"Call me black, call me blue, call me any other hue but label me human. I sprung from the same soil which brung all under this sun. I bet you never intended earning your strips rather than inherit it from man strife. Believe me boy when I tell you my blood red like 10 burning sun, like fart stench. Listen boy, without you even begin I already know why you mouth stretch out long so"

With a lean in his step he invaded my space with his breath. Oww! Horrid! "He was right bout the stench, I thought, but let me entertain him for sport. Maybe in feeling sorry for him I might in turn feel better about myself. He seemed gifted with words, coming at me with couplets disguised as madman slurs, grabbing my attention. Speaking haphazardly, jumping topics without my intervention.

"Know yourself, boy, know yourself, boy! How's your mama, spoiled boy, your teeth still have mama milk, you mad or lazy!"

It was getting late as I regretted entertaining this man in the first place. I continued to chew on the cassava bread, hurrying, trying to signify my haste, anxiously awaiting a bus. He spoke all over the place and I was taken by the wealth of knowledge and his genuine enthusiasm as he questioned me on work and other matters. Yet as he continued prying I become irritated.

"You is a police man!" I said jovially. "Why you asking me questions so?" He didn't waste any time in responding.

"Sometimes I get carried away. We is one, you know all of us connected without wires, but we all connected. So talking to you, although I've never meet you before, there is something about you - I can't put my finger on it, but you remind me a lot of...."

I cut him off with, "So you is de latest man on de street that does con stupid man!" I proceeded to raise my voice just as I finished the cassava bread, feeling a little sustained my voice now becoming a bass barrel tone, evidence of my growing annoyance and my disinterest. "What you call yourself, a cassava bread vendor slash street orator? I bet you have all de answers in the scruffy head of yours." Going on intentionally, doing my best to humiliate him, trying to make him smaller than he already is. Wishing that he would just leave.

"Choops."
He'd had enough and I could see it in his eyes.
"Is that so...Mr. know. If you as smart as you suppose, how comes your shoes venting your toes.

As I hastened past expecting no reply.

"Cause those are the toes that show strife."

Lingering on his last word I was taken by the depth of the statement or the lack thereof. I slowly halted to an about turn as if loose change fell from my holey pocket.

He continued, "Is people like you who age to be bitter like me, bitter like tjitjima, hard like stale rock cake."

"Who is this man anyway?" Trying to catch myself, resisting the pull.

"What you know about anything, anyway? What you know about anything? You tink all these words will protect you from dem clutches? You worse off than me, beating your chest like an ass."

"Move le'me pass!"

He brushed me with his shoulder as he passed, but he might as well have struck me with his cutlass. I felt cold, like endless rain was coming down and I couldn't shelter. Like I was left immobile, trying to catch myself, falling endlessly into this void of questions left unanswered for so long and at the same time drowning in this pool of new ones.

"Who is this figure?'
"Jah!"
"How is me ah?"
"Who send you?"

All this time consumed by my thoughts, this man, now horizon far rolling away with his trolley down the street like a man on a mission. Like someone sent him, he done, so he gone. My head swelled, ready to drop to the surface like a dry coconut on de pavement that supports all this rubble that has me lost in this space.

CHAPTER 9

I recalled the name and had heard a lil bout the figure. One of our more famous street dwellers or ex street dweller, he didn't look homeless to me; Nicky Blues, known around for his intense public displays of self-analysis, almost sometimes speaking as if in an out of body experience, astral projecting, looking at himself, talking to himself, amusing passers-by with his flamboyant display of language littered with variations of moans: malignant moans as if enjoying his apparent suffering. He had quite a reputation in the town as I had heard and judging from his accent, I could tell he either wasn't from here or had spent a long time in one of them bigger islands; he seemed to have inherited their rhythm in speech as he sang when he spoke, flowing along effortlessly, his tongue disconnected from his brain, just releasing rhyme, connecting words in vain. I had forgotten how much of an adventure the ville can be, all the surprises that it held, with all those characters hustling, making dough rise under this heat.

If these streets could talk, they would speak of tales of triumph, restraint and overcoming innumerable odds. I grew up here, running down the streets in homemade shorts, slippers, holey draws, and with overgrown coarse hair which spun like balls on top of my dome, as I roamed. This place was everything, my world, my eyes and ears, believe it or not, as a young tyke, your immediate environment really shapes the lens through which you view society largely. This crude life left a sour taste in my mouth at an early age. This rage that I might succumb to occasionally seemed like remnants of hurt that was sown in me from before I really understood what hurt was and why my stomach was always singing with hurt, like that in the voice of Sam Cooke. He sang, 'A Change Gone', which was in response to everything that was thrown at the American Negro. At times growling, upset, mouth dry with rigor mortis, running around nonetheless, enjoying my world. We had a lot and, well I thought we had a lot. We never cried or looked down on our predicament blaming God. Nah, never remembered left as being hard. The fondest of my childhood memories was always filled with laughter; it was not until I left my mom and went to live with my grandparents, that I learnt to view differently the place I was previously, as if New Village, being infested and slum-like made those who inhabit there less than others more fortunate with their fate, inheriting wealth or land or working through a dynasty to set a solid enough foundation that would sustain the coming feet. Shit ain't even ours anyway. I sometimes marvel at how people can speak of such amenities as if it were actually theirs, as if by some sleight of hand or magic trick, they had strategically placed the land underneath their feet. Understanding that there were the haves and the have-nots is pivotal to all of us and it is especially disheartening when you happen to come from the have-nots, as if that alone would suffice as an indication of your final destination. My language was blooming with slang and ghetto terminology, all the while loving, growing and sharing.

Here nobody cares but God. I'm hanging over the sink, gently splashing my face with water, coming back to the now. I was more fortunate than most of my peers to have got a decent education and at 23 had quickly climbed the ladder and passed through 3 levels of our education system. See, education is merit in itself and if one acquires a certain level they would seem to have reached some sort of tranquil space in their life and their struggles seemed less as they had the means and could afford the basics needed to live a good life— like food, for one. I take everything back that I said. I don't want to come off like I lived some kind of desolate almost dry desert life, where a spoonful would have to carry your physical for the day and you had no choice in the matter. No, my mom did hair-braiding and cornrowing a couple years after the foreign office where she worked as a typist had left its employees deserted and on the city streets. I remember the sound of fingers hitting keys in a mad rush and the race made harmony as she would always bear emphasis on the space key after each word. I think she gave up and I can't really remember her working a steady job after then. With that, she traded the keyboard for hair, using those nimble fingers to quickly weave through hair. I would at times fall asleep watching her as she braided then burnt the ends with a white candle. I became fascinated with fire and candle wax for some reason, having to end up scratching wax off the floor the next morning. But there were also those days she was gone, from the early light of day and this light would leave and she still wouldn't be here.

Yawning, chasing the remainder of sleep from my eyes, wiping my face down. Winds chase tears and erase all fears as I come to terms with my disposition revealed by the curtains which blow as the air thrusts its way through the hole in my bedroom window.

Woooooooooooooooooooooooosssshhh.

A heavy gust blew, sending the blood red curtain toppling to the ceiling; revealing all the darkness that consumed the outside, and the outside steady calling, seeming to send me an invitation, begging for my reply.

My reply, my reply, I thought.

What does out there have for me at this hour of night? No man's hour where devils walk the streets preying on weak souls, yearning for blood that hasn't been tainted by their touch. About 9pm now and yet no sign of mom. Even though I have gotten used to her coming much later, I feel that the darkness would somehow get the best of her this time and she would be another statistic, on the 7pm news. It's hard to sleep when I have her stuck at the top of my mind and it's even harder to keep still when the unfamiliar wind keeps whispering unfamiliar tunes reminding me that yes I am alone. Desperately trying to chase this feeling of dread creeping up my spine, invading my mind. To chase the fears away besides the wind's company all I can do is sing and sing again. Wondering where mommy went, wondering where I am headed by myself.

Nothing could keep this memory out of my mind, which I would sometimes escape to. Wish I could replay you. Although I have to admit when she was here, in the house, I couldn't stand it. She, being addicted to her keyboard, sitting here like some kind of music conductor, making an annoying tacking that never went flat, and drowning everything. All night tac - tac, tac - tac. I never got used to the crackling of that damn keyboard, I remember losing lots of sleep, that damn keyboard. This is partially one of the reasons I still am unable to sleep. Only these days someone else is doing the typing. She's the one to whom I attribute my lack of sleep. I hope wherever you are you can hear me, hear my heart, mummy.

CHAPTER 10

The scene was set, magic was how it all seemed. Aromas rose from grills along the streets filling the air as the hi-fi pounded tunes from the rear; the streets were alive with music and busy mouths on the sidelines enjoying the day's catch. I was kitted out, and feeling lucky tonight, feeling like I had won the lottery all of a sudden. That was good; I finally got over that dread feeling that had been around lately. And to think all I needed was some fresh air laced with the possibilities that lingered around the place. This seafood and fish festival celebrated the diversity of life which wasted along our shores. The aroma was the catalyst to all this and the people came to eat and unwind and free-up under the influence of some good ole *soca*. There were a few bars along the street, I had to mingle in the crowd of colours swaying on the street and preceded to the last bar, where we usually hung-out and played pool.

Although my pockets weren't that heavy I was compelled to enjoy myself tonight – no fights. I had to hurry, by now Danny and Simon might already have finished a bottle. They sat at the round table to the corner of the bar. To my surprise, she was here, the same girl from town earlier. Like déjà vu. What's her name again? I approached the table cordially trying to look careless at this point. The table was looking like the party had already ended. I saw three empty wine bottles standing on the table. Having been bled dry they just stood there; translucent in their stance as they revealed a dark reddish reflection of the scene, making the bar take on a devilish red hue through their surfaces.

"Yes, boss", Danny said. I saw him tapping his cigarette in the ash tray on the table.

I sat down between Danny and her, Simon adjacent, extending his hands to give me a jam.

"Boy, what's going on with you?" Simon asked me that again.

"You know de usual work have me dem days."

"I'm happy I ain't you, doggy. Just thinking about that kind of work does make my head swell. Glad to see you in spirit though. I ran into your friend, you remember her?" extending his hands to her.

She chuckled softly under the warmly lit bar, revealing deep dimples making worm holes on each cheek while the pearls hidden in her mouth seemed to tease a smile, embracing her face momentarily with eyes which seemed to undress me.

"Yeah, we met in town earlier," I said in return, looking intensely into her eyes, communicating forbidden nothings to her, wanting her to know I'm on to her. The scents around me must have aroused me to the point that I just gave in. I was at the mercy of the night. She made for a spectacle, fitting herself in that tightly packed red devil of a dress which hugged her soft and firm, under them warm lights driving my focus away.

"So you finally come out the cage. What have you been up to, Dread, and don't tell me its work."

I took a deep breath, dreaded having that question at me again as I murmured with my exhale, "I just been thinking bout stuff."

"What kind of stuff?" he asked.

"Private stuff."

"Since when it too private for your dogs? In fact, let me not entertain that talk right now, we have business to attend to. I wanted to show y'all a scene but before, we have a guest to entertain."

I looked over to Danny, he wasn't even here. I mean, he was here in the physical but his mind was gone as I stared at him taking totes on his cigarette, inching, inching away to an epiphany. I stared, his eye bloody, turning to recognize my stare then gone again. Simon looked charged alright. We spoke for a while, just Keisha, Simon and I. He bought another bottle and we went on. She was coming on strong and didn't seem to dig Simon's playboy lingo. *My amigo, the playboy like the Pied Piper, the soprano always knowing what cord to hit to have dem drop their draws.* Tonight something must be wrong, for while he spoke, she played footsey with me under the table and I just went along. Mind in a different place, thinking, racing again, but calm and feeling great, taking everything in, inhaling all the aromas as the wine lubricated me. What a night it's going to be.

"Oh, I almost forgot."
"Can we be excused?" Simon said to her politely.

She looked at me and said, "What y'all doing later?"

"I dunno," I said.
I looked at her puppy dog eyes and said, "I'm at their will."

"You poor thing," she said going along.

"Well, we in the club later so if you wanna see us… I mean him; he'll be in the club", returned Simon. She clutched her purse and stood up, stumbling slightly as she took her first few steps in those heels. Already she seemed possessed by the spirits as the liquor made her slur some words past me. She turned and walked out. Oh that turn! I took a long stare, thinking a body like that would really mess with a fella head, as I gulped up my drink savoring every moment.

To my dismay, Simon spelt out this place he'd been scoping for a while now. As he filled us in I could see Danny's eyes rage even more furious under the night's growing spiral.

He said to me, "Dread, I know how it is by your side dem days for money and I know what you going through. I working but it dread on my side these days. So much so, dread, that I in survival mode all now so."
He continues speaking at me but eyeing both of us.
"You hear de vibes?" he continued insistently.
"No harm."
"I would never put any of our lives in danger," he went on. I soon slipped back into this not caring feeling as I quickly agreed to go along, not wanting to feel dread again and mess up my whole night. I was out tonight and I intended on making it a night!

CHAPTER 11

We hung like ole times and I was more than happy to be there. None under the sun understands me like my inner circle; no one truly knows my pain like these two. Although we walked different paths through life we had maintained our boyhood friendships up to this point. Who knows what the future exposed? So we drank and shared our woes as if it was our last night together. Somehow I got that strange feeling then; I usually get that feeling when everything seems to go perfect. Anyway…

It was getting late and it now appeared that Simon and Danny might not be conscious enough to enjoy the rest of the night. By now they were past drunk but still seemed eager to go to the club. For a minute I had forgotten completely about Simon's proposition. He must have grown really desperate in these few months. It was the last thing I would expect of him. He and Danny seemed to have gotten rather close; I felt like I had somehow managed to fall out of orbit and lost my friends. My job had threatened the existence of everything, what remained was a dysfunctional social life and an ever thinning relationship with my girlfriend. Still, I hadn't made any real progress. I sensed Danny's influence in this whole scheme but to what extent, I couldn't tell. Simon the playboy seemed morphed, turned into something entirely different overnight. Seeing him gobble up that liquor, the way he did, did it for me.

Settled people can't fathom the pressures on a young mind in these trying times. Being bombarded daily with everything you can't have really causes one to question the fairness of things in this sphere. As the years climb and dreams recede further from your grasp you fall into this disenchanted state where all kinds of thoughts creep in. Life can be unforgiving on the man living for the fringes. The hustle can have you grow muscle but can also put a ton of strain on the young brain. I've witnessed too many of my friends get lost in the ways of the world and as a result adopted the "by any means necessary" attitude and become driven solely by the acquisition of things, big toys, shiny things, cars, jewelry, currency; any of the many external attributes that will contribute to or give the hint of success on their part. We all want to win, some by any means, it's not our fault. We were bred into this instant gratification world. These crumbs that are left for us to fight over hardly fill our tummies. We want piece of the pie, we want to bake our own pies. Don't ask why, we as a people, having been denied for so long, patience has vacated our waiting rooms which are now occupied by desperation. You see the news, you hear the statistics, shit is bad everywhere. Shit's been dark yet we see a small minority getting fat and flashing new demons on wheels every some odd month. While some of us toil so hard under the sun and can't even afford our basic amenities let alone a transport; reconditioned or used ones exceed our reach.

While on the queue to enter the club Simon and Danny decided to call it a night and asked if I'd drop them home. Seeing I was now adamant on clubbing tonight, they didn't try to put a closure on my night. I'd drop them home and one of them would pick up the rental at the office in the morning. Without a hint of hesitation I accepted and before you knew it I was in a mad rush up the highway after dropping them off. On my way back to the club, I sped through the inky night, no red traffic lights in sight, only my headlights and the reflectors on rail guards guiding my flight, solo in the rental jeep cutting the night like a knife, sporting my sharpest gear, anticipating the unfolding of the remainder of the night.

CHAPTER 12

Under the influence of the night I sat there posted at the bar, taking it all in, chasing my worries away with my *compadre* Jack Daniel. Trying to find the meaning of life at the bottom of a glass, one hand in my pocket the other maneuvering the glass like a seasoned alcoholic, playing it cool observing the scene while all the other men frolic. I already know why I'm here; my subconscious drove me on the account of a red dress a she devil sported, conspiring against me, plotting my demise. What will become of me tonight? Will I give into the chase and fall prey to her grace? I couldn't help but freeze-frame her figure, the liquor only making my desire to see her stronger, my mind further away from my empress who lay helpless at this point. If she only imagined what was going through my mind I know she'd be reduced to tears, always reducing to tears. Anything her loudmouth girls told her she would drink straight with no chaser. I bet they're in this club right now, I can feel their eyes all over me, and none would dare reveal their identity under the mystique of the flashing lights. They all hate me on account, they say, I can't be trusted. I ask you, who can really be trusted?

My history will be the death of me. I'm no longer that man but the thrill of the chase always seems to lurk over my shoulders. I made a promise to Shari and I haven't defaulted yet, regardless of the many skirts that still intrude my view. The church's pew and the mosque' Islamic themed rug have seen me more than my friends have lately; both sides of the spectrum, from either side of my parents. I try to depart from my promiscuous ways and start something that leaves remnants, a love similar to what I felt for my mother. A new, ever growing love, like that I feel for the written word. I think I love her like a metaphor, but I'm afraid of what that might mean for me. You can't teach an old dog new tricks. I'm just doomed to resort to my old ways — or can I just be patient and await Shari's warmth? I know all too well how she feels about me, how undeniable her allegiance is. That's partially why most of her loudmouth girlfriends hate me so much. They hate that she would see something in me worth fighting for, through all my bullshit, through all the drama with all those other girls who enticed me and who fell victim to my charm. All is partially my fault; the v-shape was the catalyst. I know the obsession is evident, seconds count me down after a fix, and then I want more. I can't refrain from the allure; I was predisposed to it, my old man passed it down to me through his DNA which helped shape me. Forgive me mommy, I know too well the pain a man can inflict on a woman and yet I chose to do the same. Who's to blame? No harm no fowl. I just wanna dance anyway; what's the harm in a little dancing?

To think that this hall was once vacant, left naked without a sound, without feet prancing around and without drinks being spilled. By day an empty hall, home to critters and all, dormant, dark and lonely; by night risen, loud and packed with eager souls sweating out their woes to tunes and quenching thirst with spirits that arouse coordinated chaos. The extent we would go to shed our civilized skin, just briefly, for a few hours of ecstasy.

Though we hustle we still escape and party. Though we tussle amongst ourselves still we huddle together around the ambiance of flashing lights, reenacting ancient rituals, as we assemble fashionably late in the midst of sweaty dancers, dressed spiffy - on to exercise our magnetic duties. The duties of motion, of communion; congregating under the auspices of the now and freeing ourselves, completely hidden from society behind these soundproof doors. Amongst those that communicate without the harshness of word, expressing rhythmically what we feel instinctively. I was home and the feeling that I longed for was now slowly creeping up from behind as I scanned the club looking for the bait which drew me.

Gyrating to pulsating tunes, speakers chanted frequencies and we the clubbers reenacting a ritual that we were unaware of in our naiveté. Liberating our bodies with motion, in unison with partners, and high off the sheer ambiance and hypnotized by the flashing lights marking patterns on our bodies, piercing our souls with their lasers.

I was a couple glasses of wine ahead, entering the club under the auspices of an unknown driving force. I had no control of my faculties or my body at this point. I submitted completely and utterly to the spirits within now making their dominance felt.

Suddenly my phone vibrated. Shari on the other end. I hadn't answered any of her BB messages today, I been so out of it. I couldn't answer, not right now, in the midst of all that noise and festivity. What would she think? Oh, well, I'll message her later or something.

My mind couldn't help but linger onto Shari. I wonder what she's up to now, probably she's just going to sleep. Poor thing, she's been working so hard preparing for her finals. Law school has been nothing but weathering on her. Lately she too, I suspect, had been questioning her decision to join the legal profession. I held notions, envisioning her asleep with a book in her lap. She always calls me to get away from the legislation and contractual clause for a little laugh or two.

CHAPTER 13

Suddenly while at the bar, as if by accident, my eyes drawn to the prize. I wasn't alone in my gaze, for others couldn't refrain. She took the place by storm. Solo, in the center of the club where she performed. With eyes the size of saucers I stared without a blink. I stared intently as she maneuvered the beat, as if reenacting an ancient dance choreographed by chance, her legs swaying as the beat played. She made motions across the floor, her batteries seeming eternal as she paced, hesitating to give anyone a wine. Next to me I could see a faint highlight of this man moving to the rhythm that played— in one hand a glass, in the other smoke escaping the burning furnace of a cigarette. I stared through the smoke as it intruded my view of the dancer with educated feet and lubricated waist. I myself was busy, lost following her motions, dying for a taste. Lights flashed for a second revealing her face, as her hair glowed, glittered with gold dust sweat, not wet, simply settling on the surface of her face and I waiting for the light to once again give insight to this figure. All this as I became lost in the chaos of the club.

The smoke now becoming unbearable to my eyes as it tarnished the figure on which I gazed. I moved to the bar to refill my glass, now empty after tease sipping most of the night like a man lost, savouring every drop each time, familiarizing my senses, every time thirst crept in. Damn, I hate it when the club is cluttered with thirsty, half drunk, sprung of music clubbers who couldn't give a damn about the neighbour to the side, leaning slightly on the bar trying to hide the fact that they're drunk. Without warning she approached me, having recognized me, under the lights.

"What took you so long?" she said.

She spoke to me softly in my ear, I couldn't hear, but I felt her aright. I felt her in more ways than one as the bass from the song rose, oh yes, I felt her body vibrating, skin-to-skin friction as it spoke to me in a rhythmic language and her words soft and sweet as they touched my ear, warm and wet and saying something that were not words, *"please, take me there"*. She then grabbed my butt-cheeks making them hers as I felt a surge of energy rushing to my body. We danced till I felt time stand still. Soon after, heights got escalated. It was getting late. Then, as if we both were entranced, we communicated telepathically, and then we were ghosts, disappearing in the dark. I led the way out, she held onto my hands from behind, only sweat lay between our hands. The temptress always finds you when you are most vulnerable, then distracting you, hijacking your thoughts, infesting your mind with the unclean. This defeats the purpose of this journey. Only the strong will survive and just as the thoroughbreds are those who lead, the same tune is sung by those in possession of the keys. I know better, but for now something else was in control.

CHAPTER 14

One night under the influence is equivalent to a 747 direct trip to heaven. The pain metabolizes to gain as we inch closer to this unsustained healing. My tongue anticipates its warmth as my mind springs up like an interrupted dreamer—pardon me mimicking my seniors. Tracing always seems destined to this bottle; the catalyst for my mischief, lookin' at its surface refract moon light while her dress meets the surface of grinded stone, which in the daylight resembles gold.

I was just tryin' to trace and the allure kept me. The fix re-familiarizes me with emotions void of pretenses, feelings escaped naked in the gaping south of my dome and let out everything the subconscious froze. Back and forth, without remorse our motions catching infections. Letting it all out still makes it worse but I can't refrain from confession. Although after the moment it hurts.

Symptoms of insanity, Keisha spoke to me in the same frequency so we left the scene— the dreaded, congregated, club scene. No bullshit, we skipped the foreplay and just frolicked away from prying eyes. We met our peaks and descended reluctantly as gold dust made contours of our naked frames – hand crafted by the splashing waves.

How does one come back after such an act and say to the other it was meaningless? How could I have expected things to go so far, so far was my heart and simultaneously I was so close to utopia that I just lay there? Keisha, at this point clenched on to me on the naked sands without words to distort the obvious. For a minute I got lost in the wrestling waves as they murmured cryptic messages to an intimate audience of two. I'd seen this scene before, this is the part of the night where the stars in all their majesty and mystery remind you of the sheer spectra that life is and the darkness surrounding you doesn't look all that scary but inviting like a giant pleasure sheet shielding you off from everything, making the struggles and the pain and the confusion oblivious to emotions that persisted through nature. The sea breeze blasted and we were not ever less thermal, instead just taking in the scene, hanging on to whatever brought us here in the first place. I kissed her on her forehead and told her thanks for sharing this evening with me, it seemed that the liquor was leaving my system and the gentleman in me began to make his debut. She didn't make a sound but just took my hand and put it around her. I could tell we were both somewhere else at this point. She sat in my lap half naked facing the sea, staring into the beyond. I held her until I forgot what time was, as the moon made a big impression on the evening sky, taking in this panoramic view without having to pay any fees or standing in line. The shores were ours. I'm selfish enough to want it all to myself. To make things even more spectacular, suddenly, in an instant, as if God had snored, thunder roared and rain poured. We were hopeless romantics thinking we would just sit there and pretend we won't be deterred. We dressed hurriedly; she slipped on her red dress and I pulled up my jeans and laced my timberland boots, grabbed the remainder of the wine and ran to the jeep. To think if I had stayed home like the norm I would have missed out on the possibilities of this night.

We didn't even speak as I drove up the highway. I was out of it but my eyes still gleamed and I was already contemplating my next move as we made our descent up the wet highway. I was all sobered up at this point; in fact I could use something soothing on my stomach, maybe a cocoa tea or some porridge would settle things just right. I dropped Keisha off. We exchanged numbers and I hurried down a lonely street to see if I could get something to eat.

CHAPTER 15

Thank God for the bus drivers that made it possible for these vendors to be in the city so late, or should I say, so early in the morning. Darkness still lingered but at that time you were lucky if you spotted pedestrians. Although the city never slept, hell would be reduced to icicles if the city slept; well I suppose this can be transposed: hell is cold to the marrow but hot on its surface, if that makes sense to you. It's no man's hour, where the freaks come out to scavenge and roam the land away from the disapproving stares of those that are 'supposedly' more civilized. The civilized are surely the sole contributors to this cesspool that makes it possible for these bottom feeders to exist. I hate the city at night; it can't help but be so brutally honest and show off its tattered legs to any who dare venture into this *concrete jungle* at this time. It's like at night she lifts her dress to reveal the scars on her legs. Broken souls litter the street corners as they idle in suspended animation, more in-tune to the realities of an ever cold world than I could possibly articulate. We the day walkers stoop to new lows. By day this place is a she serpent masquerading in suits, by night a rodent rolling in all the filth left over that not even flies would hover over. Every time I see a homeless person lost in his own world on the shitty streets, I see a story of someone who was pushed past the tipping point or someone who just happened to been dealt a bad hand. Or maybe someone who found refuge under the influence of a drug of choice and in turn became oblivious of his external decay. I never believed in the roles of judge and jury in these cases. I can't help but sympathize and feel some kinship to them; they are off-course sentients like myself, flesh and bones, fears, laughter, tears. Who knows their stories? Who can prescribe a remedy for their despair? We are all sick in some way; our differences might just come down to the prescriptions we subscribe to. Who knows, that could easily be me. Life is a sort of a walk on a high suspended tightrope, you take one slip and fall, you may walk after but never the same, you never know. I swear this week just passed I witnessed so many spikes and drops, highs and lows.

At my job they're coming for me. I can hear them whispering like paper being scrunched, plotting my demise. At home, mummy and I struggle to make feast out of can treats amongst other things. I can't help but want a better life for her, she's a strong woman who's been through so much and still is so hopeful. Hopeful about what, I don't know. She says I give her hope but hope on its own can't pay the bills. I just love it when I take her out and she pretends she doesn't like it. In her words she'd rather good old home. Hands down this is the only relationship I can count on. I feel like I'm on a raft and slowly drifting away from my closest friends. I wonder why Danny turned into this different person. He unfolded right before my eyes and all these years I was too caught up in my own affairs to even be there for him. He and Simon must have thought I had forgotten about all those plans we made and how we would start a business and build a studio together. If everything Simon and Danny say goes according to plan we can walk away with a lot and possibly change things for us. Rome wasn't built by idealists who never got their hands dirty. You know sometimes you have to pillage to grow. At this point, I'm willing to follow any leads that might see me advancing.

Chapter 16

On what was a busy side street where the ghetto and the city meet, just a couple feet from where the buses assemble, I approached a stall which stood adjacent to a useless high-wall, no doubt from a partially demolished tree in the jungle where garbage usually pilled. The wall near the food stall bore scribbles from graffiti artists, like carvings on tree trunks. I call them ghetto hieroglyphs. The artists of the day marked their domain with their aliases and profane illustrations of a shallow taste, no doubt imperfections in their illustrations, although their signatures bear hints of dexterity. As I got closer I was surprised to see it was Nicky Blues underneath the stall. I hesitated at first and then gave in, my thirst creeping in and I thought he might have spice. I'm in luck.

"Hey you, my boy!" he shouted. "Say, I remember you. What's the matter, don't tell me my cassava bread drove you here at this time."
With an inviting tone he continued along.

At this point the rain was becoming unbearable; I had no choice but to seek refuge under the stall.

"Come shelter, my boy."
"My good Lawd! What have you here at this time? I know you ain't from the city, so what drag you here?"

"Never mind that," I said in response as I peeped at the items he had on display underneath in this wooden tray, like those at a jewellery store. The stall had a simple wooden framed countertop with a little glass window about 3 by 2 feet in the center exposing the contents in the bottom, illuminated by a little light bulb that seemed to add a radiant gloss on his treats. He had four little Pyrex dishes in there, most of which were almost empty and covered with plastic wrap. One of them had cassava bread; the others had floats, Dahl and chicken wings. On top the counter he had a strange looking tablecloth, with some elaborate flower pattern like a curtain. On the counter stood about three bottles of various colours denoting the poison of choice. Through the bottles you could see the different stalks, vines and other plant portions that many would soak in the white rum which gave the '*spice*' its potency. If I was correct, I recognized by the colour he had honey spice, ganja spice and one with grenadine syrup, making the concoction a garnished watered down red. There was also a large metal flask with contents beyond my.

The rain was reduced to a dripping drizzle, we still stood under the little umbrella stall.

"How comes you out so early in the morning?" I asked, trying to change the topic.

"Someone has to feed dem hungry souls, my boy. These bus drivers work round de clock and sometimes need something tasty to chew. Sometimes they just need some spice to make them feel nice. I do my part, they support me so I've been there doing this a while now and then, until I had to build this umbrella stall. You see how it come in handy? You see how it comes in handy at times like this?"

I watched the drizzle through the street lights on the lamp post, they seemed soft like tears descending from the dark heavens making all anew. Washing all the earth's sins away so we can continue sinning another day.

"You look fresh from the slaughter!" he said nosily.

"What you mean?" I returned, thinking how I'd managed to meet him on the streets this late.

"What you think? Early morning, look at you— I done taste the alcohol on your breath and look how far you stand."

"Never mind that, just give me a spice or something warm to cool out mi self," I said sternly, singing the last words.

"Alright champ, I'll fix you up. But I ain't giving you spice, too late for that. You need some warm tea on your stomach. How about a Dahl and cocoa tea? Come on, trust me.

"Oh, alright."

"Ah, now there's a smart choice my boy."

"Ain't you Nickey Blues?" I said curiously.

"Why, yes, I must be real popular if you know who I am. I can't remember ever serving you before earlier and I never forget a face."

"Yeh, I don't usually come in town like I used to and I don't really buy things from street vendors."

"Well your preference not mine, buh I bet I'm no less hygienic then all dem big restaurants in de city."

"I suppose, but it's not really that."

"Anyway my boy, here you go and relax, de drizzle will be over soon."

He continued, "Ain't nuttin better in this shallow place than a warm cup of cocoa tea to make you forget about the rain or the pain, whichever reign."

"It's something else, isn't it?"
"Been here from bout 9 and without notice de rain just suddenly creep up on me. It's strange, just an instant downpour, not even a slight drizzle, just full force like dem balloons up dere just buss."

"Yeh, sometimes it just happens like that. I suppose I rather it happen like that than a continual drippin drizzle that seem to never cease and just make everything more unbearable than they already are."

"Oh, I see. But something tells me you referring to more than just de weather dere my boy."

"What gave you that idea?"

"Why, the way you put it, you make it sound so personal— I would even go on to say you using the rain as a symbol for something. Well, my boy, if that's the case I bet that's a taste, is it, just a little taste of what going on in that big head of yours."

I felt rather composed around him at this point, like I could tell him anything. I could discourse with him aright. His composed demeanor made him inviting to talk to. Extending my hand I grabbed the plastic cup, feeling warmth in my hands as I slipped the other in my pocket, handing him a note.

"That's for now and you can keep the rest. Sorry about yesterday, I haven't been feeling like myself lately," I said.

"Nonsense, keep it, your money's no good here." As he continued I could sense an interrogation session coming along. I felt willing and compelled to let the now reign supreme at this point as the liquor in me seemed to be making its exit. I felt a sense of rationality slowly prevailing.

CHAPTER 17

"Can I ask you something?" I said, taking a sip of the hot tea.

"Shoot"

"Have you ever felt like you… ah never mind."

"Come on…go on."

"Ah never mind. I ain't want to burden you."

"Nonsense my boy, what's on your mind?" asked said.

"If you insist. Have you ever felt like you ain't living to your fullest or like something's weighing you down and you can't quite put a finger on exactly what it is, something you cannot account for and it have you feeling like you missing out on something?" I felt the need to go on and attempt to let out all what's been taxing on my faculties lately, right this very minute. I had a great night and felt compelled to make this morning's wee hours something different. I had no sleep in my eyes even though I danced my ass off and then some more. He was reduced to ears as I went on. I continued.

"I dunno, buh ah exactly here I thought I wanted to buh now I just feel like running away. I just want to start anew. I feel like me against the world right now, for some strange reason. I just want to go somewhere it's warm, where my dreams assimilate flight."

He cut me off just as I was going to continue, stretching his beard saying, "Listen, listen, listen!" he said hurriedly. "First things first. What do you do, I mean do you work or go to school?"

I broke down my credentials and background, not really thinking he would understand me but surprisingly he seemed to have already figured out that I wasn't his average customer.

"My boy, you must be really smart, ah."

"I suppose." I said unenthusiastically.

"Le'me feel you in on a little secret. There's nuttin really new under the sun, they just dressed different but I bet you they all serve the same purpose."

"What you mean?" I said. I felt rather intrigued at this point and wanted him to expand on what he just said.

"What I mean is ain't nuttin wrong wit you that ain't already affected someone else. Doesn't matter if you have a BA, BSc, MSc or a, how dem fellas get to call demselves doctors, with PhDs. We all breathe the air and all our hearts pump blood. A lil advice from an older head: whatever problems or situation you going through the best remedy is to put it down in some fashion. Write it, or draw it or paint it, talk it, shout it, sing it. Trust me, for you, I reckon you seem smart enough."

He continued in a more serious tone. "Put it down in words, it may sting more but I guarantee you it will go a great deal far in helping. I ended up alone a long time ago because I got afraid and like most men do, I ran. I left my responsibilities and I ran. And I've learned that you can't run fast or far enough, sooner or later karma's gonna *com-a-knockin*."

"So you not Lucian. I thought so, your accent gave it away but I wasn't sure."

"Nah man I come here from Jam town a while back, back when I didn't have this full beard or all these scars on mi arm. Trust me, my boy, I can give you firsthand account of de repercussions of running away."

"Since I been here I've hurt in my heart and I regret the day I ran away. See, this thing here's hard and some compromises are necessary. I wasn't gonna compromise my freedom. I had so many ideas I hoped would bear fruit. I can't say I didn't try, I just got frustrated with bureaucracy, hypocrisy all neatly dressed in formal attire. I assumed the demeanour of a law practitioner. I believe in the law and due process but I soon realized that justice was awarded to those who could afford it, leaving the rest at the mercy of the courts.

I remember like it was yesterday, spending mi mommi hard-earned money on everything besides school. From my second year at university I was never the same and assumed total disinterest in law, academics and so many other social constructs composing this system. Looking back at it, time seem to fly by so fast. I went from sleeping in class to sleeping in the streets, not knowing where I woke up. I good with my hands and my Muh taught me early how to bake and stew and fry so I began giving back with what she left me with. God bless her soul. She wasn't even five feet, a pygmy, handling six of us and to think the oldest one, the one who'd shown so much promise would desert everyone and run and hide. Actually I didn't run at first, see, I was chasing tail, one in particular, a Lucian daughter from de valley. Shabin and thick! But she gon' now and I was left here to scuffle for me self. Ain't never called home nor write, I can't bring myself to see Mama disappointed."

CHAPTER 18

He went on for what seemed like days, punctuating every once in a while for a sip of spice and a cigarette drag. I listened quietly, finishing my Dahl in deep meditation as his story unraveled. I caught slight similarities along the way, wondering what the real cause was of this man's choosing to roam the dirty city streets selling things outta this stall. He seemed articulate and smart enough for a regular work. His beard covered his face with aggression, marking a nappy trail that disappeared under his shirt neck.

He wore what appeared to be an old limp trench coat, patched together in pieces shaped like continents, all appearing in different hues under the auspices of the street light, patched up in different threads. He didn't look the least bit scathed, sporting his coat like it was one of those designer coats, elaborately done, like those threaded jeans you buy fashionably torn. It looked like it was all over the place and fitted him well though, tailored like he sewed every patch together himself. Some of the patches looked more worn out than others. He stood a good six feet from the ground, coffee black, broad shoulders, with a chiseled face with facial hair that covered his face. Sportin' an old thick cotton bell bottom pants about shin high, bloody red dark vertical lines and one of those black caterpillar boots you'd find on workers on construction sites. I didn't feel the need to comment on his dress, as that would just get him going. Besides, his attire showed a character far from the customary. I would put him in his late forties and if my calculations were correct without evidence of any grey hairs my calculations might have some weight. He stroke his beard lightly, playing with the nappy balls making them straight, stretching them as he continued speaking.

I had become quite fond of him, drinking out the steaming cup not noticing how much I'd told him. Not even noticing I had told him all the plans I had laid out in my head, about Shari and I walking down the aisle together and of all my other dreams and aspirations, pursuing my interest and building a life, everything except the white picket fence and all that mellow *domesticado* us simple folks hope to acquire. And he listened, seeming quite amused, like he knew of something either I hadn't discovered or wasn't privy to at this juncture. His eyes glared, seeming to reflect on something distant, mutely communicating prescient truths as I lay my story down on the canvas. While the steam from the cocoa tea rose into my nostrils, inhaling the brew with a hint of ginger, we were going on with only the few street lights, him and the empty, stationed buses as witnesses. Me opening up to him now, opening up like some gutted fish, exposing all my insides to this man… This man whom I hardly knew but who seemed to know me all right, seemed to accept me although I was so disrespectful. Being hesitant at first played no part in him helping me out, absorbing my tale, he playing the role of an unorthodox shrink, me assuming my normal confused state. Now lubricated off the tea my mind quietly fled from all those fantasies of mine, as I attempted to decode this figure before me.

"You see, can I call you, Nickey? By the way, why, is that your real name? Why folks call you Nickey Blues?"

"I see you really ain't from de city now. I'm de original blues man. My name is Nicolas, but I is ah blues man at heart. Nina Simone, Nipsey Russell, Sam Cooke, all dem men have nuttin on me. I used to sing at the market steps after hours serenading passers-by, infecting folks with my blues. I love de blues; I think de blues is de truest, man. No other music gets down to the marrow of things like de blues."

"Is that so? I know blues die a long time ago."

He returned in an angry tone. "Nonsense, my boy, de blues cah die. And all this time I thought you was smart. How can blues die, that's just like saying calypso can die. My boy, blues is de sorrow and de pain of de people expressed lyrically. Blues is the truest expression there is. I know you is one of dem young fellas from de new school, you into de hip hop, dub and RnB vibe but if wasn't for blues dem music wouldn't be. Listen my boy; I know exactly why you feeling so. See, you young fellas used to listening to mun sing bout gurls and fancy things and all that camera things your TV brings. But blues is exactly what the world need at this point. You have to get out of that fantasy you living and express all that you goin through. How else, my boy, you'll get help in dealing with life? De new generation, I cah understand dem fellas for the life of me; they tink that reading some book and separating themselves from what really is important will make all their troubles disappear."

"I ain't like blues music, that's ole timers ting. Besides our music express our woes and struggles, too!"

CHAPTER 19

"Anyways my boy, carry on smartly, buh that veil you have hanging over you pales your insight, the picture you see is not what is actually. You see what you want, not what is. Your mind deceives you! Your mind seems like it doesn't want to come to terms with the true nature of things. Let me tell you, boy, I was once a little dreamer like you, hoping that one day if I worked hard enough my dreams would come true. I was blinded by my own desire and driven by my thirst for all that I see. I was driven by the allure of all these things that call you. All that which makes you aspire to reach new heights, all that makes it possible to attain those things that only those you see at the top desperately hold on to."

He was really starting to piss me off at this point, talking all that blues talk and condescending talk, like he knew something I didn't. I had to come back swinging; this was turning into a real informal debate; I was more than willing to continue the exchange and see where it led me.

"What do you mean, and what are these things that you think I'm drawn to? You must be confusing me for one of your customers who frequent your stall, hoping to get more than a cassava for purchase. Look at me, I hardly fit the description of any of them. Who else you know is battling with everyone and is challenged by no one? Who else you know is far from that which they claim and as a matter of fact, who else would waste their time talking to some ole reject? You are rejected from society because you don't fit into the norm. Look at you; your attire, your appearance. Trust me, if you want to get people to pay attention to you have to do something about that body odour of yours. It's a force field that keeps people away and prevents you from ever making contact."

"Pay attention!" he hollered in surprise, thumbing his cigarette. "You think I give a rat's ass about what people think or what people pay attention to? My boy, look around you. This circus that surrounds you doesn't give a rat's ass about you, so why don't you return the favour? Understand that we are here because we have been dealt by the hand of God, not by some deliberate scheme created by man to keep us slaving for this bread."

I fed myself every syllable of what he said, not because it was the gospel but because it was illuminated with truths that I seemed hesitant to embrace although I had been all too familiar with the true nature of things.

"I have no control over anything around me. I am at your will; you hold me down and give me life. Your interest in my tale, besides, I am a reject, right? An ole dirty, smelly, reject who couldn't cope and because of that I am banished from that world you call your own, that world you claim will accept you even if you detour from the path that it chose? My boy, I myself can't understand it at times, and now at my age don't even want to begin to understand it. All I see is this cycle of darkness manifesting itself in de multitude of ways that subscribe to our desires. I thirst, you know? You think is you alone that want all you see? The difference between us however is I understand why these things are there and the purpose they serve. Nothing here is granted, nothing there is eternal and I guarantee you that nothing here can make you feel full."

I glanced at him; he seemed to be on a pulpit speaking to a congregation of lost, hungry souls. His reverence escaped all his attributes that would discredit him and for a brief moment I was faced with a man who no longer was bound by the things which held his jaw and muzzled his freedom. Instead I was looking in a mirror, a mirror showing me that which I couldn't see. Like a scar on your back, although it's healed and the pain is gone it leaves a mark that will forever be with you and that mark holds the memory of its inception and it's pain and somehow holds the clue to everything around you. You forget it, well, until your hand makes contact with the scar or you take a glance at it in the mirror or an inquisitive friend attempts to uncover the story behind the scar.

My mind raced far, further away from where we stood, away from the feeling that held me for as long as I could remember. Hope escaped me briefly as I became lost in deep thought.

"The darkness?" I said

"Yes, the darkness my boy! Don't you see it? Everything is clotted with a layer of darkness; d'evils that decorate the life and add flavour to the light. Don't you know that it runs this place and our love for it is the reason that it has become this praised. It's everywhere, from the street corners to the corner shops, from the board rooms to the court rooms, down to the cell block and the street block; none can escape the plot. So as it has been written, so shall it be, so don't expect anything but what you see. He who controls the darkness runs things and animates everything. Our desires grow from his footsteps, he is the one that they follow; ask them, they will deny but he is the one they march with. The fiends rush for his touch and kill for this. Trust me, nuttin will stand in the way of man and his vices."

CHAPTER 20

"But Nickey, then what you saying is that nothing here really matters and we shouldn't bother ourselves working this hard and saving up or none of that. Think about it, I see nothing wrong with wanting these things I desire, they add value to my life and these things say I've reached a level where I have the right to enjoy these little pleasures. We people push ourselves not because we want to buy things but it's the human nature to strive for better."

"My boy, think about it. Think 'bout what really matter at the end of the day, subtract all the petty and vain desires and things. After you done all that subtracting, see how many of dem things you really need."

He paused, then added, "Think bout it. What matters?"

A persistent car alarm erupted in the background. He continued.

"Being satisfied, hardly ever. Just when you thought you were through, another lever appears. Climbing up a never ending ladder - for what? Just to be satisfied? Where does it end? Do you follow? Just to be reduced on your trot! Then what? How far are you willing to go? Can't you see? It will never be enough. No amount will ever satisfy the urge."

I lack that urge to amass on account of thinking of myself as more than just a machine, though it seems to be how I'm reduced to at present and to be quite honest I don't want or need the baggage that comes with amassing. People conspiring, don't get me started. I wonder if others feel how I do.

"Le'me ask you, my boy. Are you satisfied? Is your soul satisfied? Does that fire I see hidden deep in those eyes ever engulfed your face with rage, or joy, or laughter? After all that schooling and you still can't sustain a joyful thought for the duration of a day. Contented with simply surviving after all dem people fight for you. Convenient amnesia, ignoring your past, your heritage, falling into *they* trap, chasing what? Chasing some feeble ideal that so fine it can float in the wind? What bout all dem people who die so you can be here? You tink they die just for you to buy things and make money? My boy, the picture is bigger than all of that, you're blinded by what you're fed; I can't blame you or your generation. All that talk of y'all have it hard – you ain't know the first ting about having it really hard or having to fight for anything. You so used to being spoon-fed that you dun forget how to feed yourself."

"You know what really matters?", he continued.

"Doing the things you love, being around people you love while everyting's intact, helping your people, carrying on the tradition that was left for you. My boy, don't get caught up. Hell, I would never trade a soul for gold or stoop to pick up mun poop. I would never give away dem memories. However rough dem times, boy, dem memories worth more to me than me ladi. And cost more cause I paid in mostly sweat and tears, had no metals so my presence chase all leeches and bitches. People testing you to see if you testable and if you squirm like a worm, you know they coming back. Why you tink you have that fight in you? Why you tink you always want to hit something? My boy, you have that fight in you, you from a strong people. Deal with everything now and get it out before it too late. I believe that's what's wrong with this godforsaken place. Nobody taking time to wrestle with de real questions, everyone just want to live nice and happy and keep ignoring that voice inside them. Nobody wants to sing de blues. Is your soul that speaking dere you know? I is a blues man, so is my soul that speaking dere. That's why I tink am a compulsive talker of the sort, my soul always leaking, oozing out blues. De bluest blues, my boy! I need a smoke."

He placed his hand in his pocket and pulled out a Benson pack, removed the last two cigarettes out and said, You safe, you want one?"

"Nah mun, I kool."

He lit one in his mouth and placed the other in the pocket of this trench coat.

"That's another thing, the smoking and drinking is we kryptonite. Dem things just dere to extinguish us, my boy."

He took a long drag and exhaled through his nostrils.

"Look at how de blues have me, de bluest blues boy. Sometimes I just like to be in another place, sip mi spice, smoke a little and just sing to me heart's content."

CHAPTER 21

He seemed to be taken over by whatever he was under as I saw him pour himself another plastic glass of spice and leave the back of the stall to come join me in the front. Suddenly, without any request or invitation, he began to sing.

♪

But that's the whole tragic point, my friends
What would I do if I could suddenly feel?
And to know once again
That what I feel is real
I could cry
I could smile
I might lie back for a while
Tell me what, what would I do if I could feel?

What could I do if I could reach inside of me?
And to know how it feels to say I like what I see
And I'll be more than glad to share all that I have inside of here
And the songs my heart might bring
You'd be more than glad to sing

♪

He breaks out hysterically in a shrieking sound, imitating Nipsey Russell that would force the dumb to holler in distress. He got this point across alright and was more than caught up in the moment, as I watched, not knowing whether to be bewildered, terrified, or engaging.

He is probably there for a reason, you know, in that state. That state where once you cross there's no way back to shore. I swear my eyes were deceiving me, him twirling and moving like some kind of a crazy *toppie,* spinning with no sense of direction; frantic. He then hollered from the top of his voice, so loud that the birds in the air heard his despair.

♪

And if tears should fall from my eyes
Just think of all the wounds they could mend
And just think of all the time I could spend
Just being vulnerable again
O tell me what, what, what would I do?

♪

He being his own choir of course.

He was right. But that's the whole tragic point, he hit the nail squarely. What would I do, if I could suddenly feel and to know once again that what I feel is real? I bit my tongue and the pain brought back memories that were lost under rubble in my mind. A time where things made sense and I loved coming home to a warm meal and warm hearts eager to hear how my day passed. And the years passed and time lapsed and I grew, out of mom's clutch and ran right into the wild, grew out of the childish tricks onto some real shit. I was eager to prove myself and to prove myself by any means, even if it meant detaching myself from the very place which shaped me, watered me and watched me grow...All I know is that in order to distinguish myself from all the filth surrounding me and everything clouding my vision I had to isolate myself, even if that isolation was from my very foundation, well, that would just have to be the case. It was; and I shut all doors and went into hibernating, away from all the noise and distractions and steadily reached for my goals. I thought for sure that a degree and all the accolades that accompany it brought you to that place, where your mind's at a tranquil and everything just falls into place.

Is there even such a place? I thought. If there is, I'm far removed. This place - this place that I dwell could rival hell. Devils don't sport horns here and what's here's even more devious and mischievous than Lucifer himself. You could see them ravaging and pillaging the place, soaking everything dry. Like leeches they suck, like parasites they hang until nothing's left to feed their greed. Until the grounds are sick and the air is thick, molasses thick, with all the ills, all the ills that a "modernized society" could fill. Teenage turns parent-age and death rate turns to birth rate. And not to mention the ill fate of the ghetto youth growing, contaminated by society's ills, born a product and made a customer; manufactured fiends, *fiends* to all they see, all that their nostrils could sniff and all that salivates their mouths. Without a doubt, I was made into this being that learned and worked and strived for the little that I have. And (with) these little gifts God has placed into my possession I will forever use them, use these hands to translate my heartbeat. Translate my feelings, my pride my joys. You never stop being a boy even if you try. The spirit lays dormant but that doesn't mean you can't raise it and let it shine and let it serve its purpose rather than forever sleeping, stifling inside; selfish with all of this creative energy, this love, this thirst for everything right and this passion for everything true. *I pray that I may not be long lost along the way; I pray that evil not come my way.* And with this I felt a surge of energy pass through my body, invading my anatomy, feeling my insides with light, tickling my senses straight. I couldn't explain this sudden rush of joy watching this man, this man prancing around, this man with nothing and supposedly everything at the same time.

And that's the real tragic point, my friends: if you want the best of both worlds you might just end up in your own world.

"Hold on!" he shouted." We don't need no more ghost, we need a song." Nickey continued, "You gotta sing more, you can't be no ghost cause you gotta be a spirit for - you gotta be a spirit!! ...And then the spirit cannot descend without...Soooonnngggg!"

"You got to be a spirit, you can't be no ghost!"

I had no idea where he was going with all this but hey, I guess that's the transformative qualities of liquor for you.

CHAPTER 22

I had gotten lost in the unfolding episode and forgot completely I had work in the morning; matter of fact work was a couple hours away. I started to hear cock crows and vehicles already starting to make their presence felt in the city at this point. I instantly bade farewell to Nickey Blues and rushed to the jeep to get home.

"Ah, wait nah! You see, my boy, ahh, I feel better already. Ah surviving the times. All you have to do is embrace de blues and make it part of your story. Don't make de blues burden you but carry de blues, exhale de blues, channel it somehow. That's why I told you to put it in words. You see, I put it in song. I guarantee you after you put it down everything will be clear. The trick to life...come closer, I ain't want nobody stealing my lil secret."

"But there's no one around."

He whispered. "Nonsense, my boy, de spirits always around. Why you think you feelin so? They dun (maintain spelling you started with)take you already.

Now listen, the trick in life is to take it how it come, do your best but take it how it comes. Imagine you swimming out to sea and a big tide coming at you bringing you back to shore, for every stroke you take the tide taking you back two. There's what you do. You do the only practical thing. You swim with the tide. My boy, there's no chance you can ever compete with nature, not only nature as in the weather, but the nature of things, the nature of people, of work; you only one person going against forces that dere way before you and will continue to be dere after you gone. What you have to do is find ways to move with the tide, my boy, just roll with things, find ways of using the forces to your advantage. If that makes any sense to you."

"For every hundred of us that get caught up in all that life throws, there are a few who master the art of things and look how successful and happy they are. By success and happiness, I ain't mean having a whole lot of money or fancy things. I mean just being a provider, just being a contributor to this game called life, no matter how small. The energy you bring forth have a lot to do with your external and internal demeanour. Then you realize that fear is the only thing you have in your way; nothing can stop you from going where you have to. ...Think about it, my boy!"

"Oh shit. What's the time?"

"It's about minutes to 4"

"Oh shit! I have work in the morning; I need to get some rest.

"But my boy, before you go on running, remember my foolish advice. I may not be decorated or certificated, but I know a few things you can't find in dem books. And one more thing, remember you ain't need nobody but yourself to make things happen, you'se your own father and your own sun; is you that have to shine, my boy, nobody else. Follow your heart and use you mind to steer away from trouble and I bet I will be reading bout you in de paper sometime soon. I ain't a psychic but I just have a feeling 'bout you. Things don't just happen, everything has its consequence, my boy, remember that."

Know the words but can't quite choose the right one. Can't quite say what's wrong but it's weighing a ton; gotta broaden them shoulders. I bent over to look at the surface and in that moment became sympathetic to its pain. Imagine sustaining so many loads.

"On the radio people busy talking about how many died today, was shot today. I wonder how many babies that was born today, drew their first breath. How many dead souls have resurrected from their slumber. We is all asleep, you know. How many people turn the honest direction? Tuned out of all that noise and taken the step in the right direction, to the light. Never mind how minute or grand, the importance is the stand. Realising something's wrong, listen to your soul and bring out some light. The darkness consumes but every spark of light is important my boy, ignite them fires. Never use it in destructive means, illuminate me, serenade our existence and shift levels of consciousness with our collective beings, sentient beings, possessors of soul. I know they ain't teach you that in school. Brought here on no accord, left for dead. I ain't finish yet, I know a little sumting."

"My boy, if you have to leave with anything, take this. Rather than anticipating death, concentrate on the living. What is it to be human, derived from the Latin word *humando*, meaning of the earth, dirt; no less inseparable from the trees. Most of us qualify as trees, standing here being swayed by words, by promised lies. Fill a container of hope and pray it will stay afloat. But you are ever deceived, still carrying on maintaining hope. When you get tired of waiting and you fill the void with a lil help from the hope pushers; selling you hope in ritual fashion."

Standing here, listening and him saying nothing. Nothing new anyways. You might have heard it all, charisma just enabled it to change tone like blues, poetry, conversation, conflict, waves bashing against the shores, laughter, crying, moans; all a reflection or averse to something, something warm, something cold, something empty or hollow. Hovering over, daunting, always to follow.

I followed with, "Ok, Ok, but I have to leave. I'll try to take what you told me into consideration."

-ACT III-

"ILLUMINATION"

(THE PRESTIGE)

Illumination

There's a sneak peek into this abstract realm where this black man dwells. Unattached and unscathed by Time's deliberate procession into days - which lie there pondering, wondering, whispering mysteries forgotten by his own recordings of histories. Histories forged and crocheted in this infinite loop, me being he, trapped by the inability to lay tracks which lead back. Back to the beginning of this sphere or even closer; to the beginning of this here. Where my feet surface.

Making sense seldom, his abilities question the rational, causing thoughts to manoeuver reality. Without a soul, this left his temple so cold. Only one goal. This goal kept him from being sane. Only one goal. That is to trace history's face and understand this fucking place.

I

No ceilings
Unlearning fears
Descending stairs.
Chasing esoteric crumbs
Conserving with bums,
Crazy winos, fashioning tales foreign to my earlobe.
Listening through walls
Watching ants feast on kids left in rubbers
Huddling over shoulders of forefathers looking for keys
Martyrs cry for babies, hovering over all'em.
Still descending
T.S. Elliot chess boxing Christopher Wallace; wasteland in the background, while Shaytan contemplates his next move. Nothing's mathematics, found in that dark following the light.

II

On a normal eve the sun stood
Illuminating as It should.
Unveil with hives, awake the lives
With slender shown on pavement stone.
Why govern with laws and then might,
Fury pierces the skies with light.
Until the battle begin anew
I bid you all *Adieu*.

Interlude

Tessellated surfaces like chessboards pave my existence; into dark and light, wrong and right, day and night. My sentiments choose this life I took, hooked to sentences with no remorse for my steed; the pen indicts men, ignites dormant furnaces ablaze. And I have to thank he who made it possible to express my feelings lyrically, literally, parallel to the truth and acute to the abstract that have men subtract the divinity and get lost in vanity. Slaves, I wish you would confront me, dressed in your formal attire, thinking I'm easily deceived like the rest of the flock. Today might be the last day you see me mild mannered, cooperative and acting in accordance with the mundane. My eyes are wide open to the travesty. Whether you confront me physically with fist or covertly with condescending lingo, bet I'll be the victor. Victory is in my clutches and the world is mine, you an ancestor, almost at the end of your run. I'm a thoroughbred, nappy head, master of the terrestrial and digital arena funded by you seniors. It's high time we stop being subservient and easily swayed by the old-fashioned big belly men who can't even bend and touch their toes, playing politics; pretending each other are foes. And behind our back they dine in expensive restaurants gulping expensive bottles of wines.

Clutter is my life; I live in the midst of confusion buried under ideas, on and off constructions, projects that may never see the light of day. I continue for the sheer joy and the dexterity it instills in me, every piece brings me closer to utopia. I envision a blacksmith spending decades in front of eternal fires mastering his craft, until he becomes the flames, maneuvering the metal at will. Or a petal whose sprout reveals the first light of Rah, revealing a unique beauty to a world that would label it ordinary. The part of the creator becoming lost in his creation suffers his ability to render his efforts justice; words do not suffice and feelings cannot be translated. The time spent can sometimes be painstaking and unkind, and the magic, when harnessed, must be somehow stretched for the duration of the construction. The creation is never perfected in the creator's eyes; it must however morph and stand on its own – to critique and scrutiny. I disagree in the judgment of any creation; it's easy to be outside of the creative sphere and cast aspersions, determining social relevance and aesthetic appeal of a labour of love, born out of thought, pollinated with heart and expressed matter- phorically.

Beauty supersedes flawless skin, garnished surfaces, chiseled features, curvature or texture of hair. Beauty is depth and beauty is sentient. Beauty is the creation in the eyes of the creator. Beauty is when we create, beauty is when we procreate, beauty is when we relate to the infinite which comes together to make us definite. Definite universal bodies of light and infinite possibilities of flight! And when I saw myself for the first time in her eyes I knew that beauty also was in the union of us two.

———

CHAPTER 23

Nicky's little monologue left me unsettled and even contributed to me waking up late. That's right, I'm late again. This time I'm anticipating the worst, I'm cursed. It was now 9:40, a new low for me, a whole hour and some late. I'm anticipating the interrogation session. As I run up the stairs the secretary stops me and directs my attention to a problem which caused the main computer server to go down. I was then told that management was trying to reach me with no success and that this downtime prevented the members of the board from retrieving their report data for their scheduled board meeting. My eyes are still red; I haven't fully recovered from last night's episode, although I slept like a baby. The receptionist also says that I am to report to the boss as soon as I enter, not a minute more.

I hesitated to his office like a student on the way to the principal, expecting punishment. It appeared that he had already been notified of my arrival, for as I opened his door I overheard him replying that I was already there. Probably the secretary, who cares! All I wanted to do this minute was be anywhere but here. I had to face it, whatever he threw at me, I had to remember that I'm at fault here and I had been awarded more chances than a cat with 9 lives. I approached his desk sternly, trying to appear alert and fully aware of my dilemma.

That man's face looks just like my face but our methods wouldn't trace, I've veered off course, to him I wouldn't relate. With him I couldn't debate, far polarized, yet I see the same fires raging in our eyes. The similarities were our eyes, they held no disguise, they gleam red with passion and his just had a tad more insight. They would blind other eyes seeking direct contact, they would tell no lies. An older me, a younger him physically, only difference was my frame towered over his, I was the athlete he never was.

As it is said by old folks, the fruits don't fall far from the tree. My case was different; it seemed that I was the stubborn fruit who rolled off course, like a rock gathering no moss. The hairs on his arms covered his brown tone with aggression, forcing, and seeking visibility from underneath his long sleeve ends where his hands began. Well defined countenance expressing anguish as he spoke, neatly marked sideburns emphasising his masculinity. Hair naturally molasses-dyed with one or two greys sticking out their pale strands; evident of experience, or an over-consumed brain that held so much financial information on investment strategies, or secret hideaway destinations for rendezvous with women who looked like calendar models with a hint of sophistication in their strut. I sat there at the moment composed, calm and taking it all in, he delivering like a seasoned actor, voicing his disappointment in me without a shred of hesitation. Excuse my arrogance but at this point in my life he couldn't faze me, what he only managed to do was raise my temperature. Like a pressurized kettle that might blow soon. It would take an elephant's tranquillizer to suppress my kettle's whistle. Suddenly he stood up to make it more dramatic, I sat there in-front his oval desk awaiting my sentence like I was on trial for something horrendous, something on the white-collar tip, like treason. I was the least bit phased on the surface; I had been there too many times. I had been crucified by him way too much. I was trying to embrace the circumstances that brought me there once again and forcing myself to feel the gravity of the situation. I was somewhere else at this point, and felt at the moment that this wasn't the place for me. He continued in his normal unilateral discourse with a tone that all the other employees dreaded but I had become quite used to. This time something was different, I looked at him dead in the eyes. All I could see was his lips moving and his hand movements with his demeanour marching his serious attire. A white long sleeve shirt with ruby cufflinks covered his top. His silk ties always complemented his tailored pants, with French loafers at the bottom that resembled leatherback turtles—but I think I had the wrong reptile, gators would be a surer bet. Anyone could tell that every item was coordinated and well thought out, unlike my choices that were spontaneously driven. All for one reason. He was one the ladies would die for and one the young and blind aspire to be: sharp, unsympathetic and well put together, with manicured fingers and pedicured toes.

His friends: the fat cats, the corporate elite, riding around in cars, topless cars, without bras. My friends: the flavoured youth, with minds sharper than a sabre-toothed predator, tattooed in graffiti, marked up like dark tunnels on highways or abandoned hallways. Our non-conformist ways saw us misinterpreted by the older folks settled in their ways. Generation Y, born in the instant gratification era, where everything revolves around on the paper. The Wu-tang Clan articulated it best: *C.R.E.A.M.* Those amongst us who had it through inheritance got appointed leaders and those who didn't had to be creative in some way or another in order to be visible. Plotting on how to make what we saw on those screens and in our dream manifest. Trying to imitate role models whose favourite pastime was drinking out of brown bottles. Hennessy dreams are what the boys on the street corners share. I never really understood their limited grasp, my dreams were way more sophisticated than the flashy over compensated ones they dreamt. I can't speak for all but the dialogue was always a repeat of the lavishes of a rap video, poppin' bottles, topless models, diamonds on their crucifixes, Jordans on their feet.

My mind was everywhere apart from where it was supposed to be, trying to escape the emotion that would eventually cripple me.

He continued then he paused briefly, catching his breath. I now descended from the vantage point of this imaginary mountain as his mouth motions turned into audible sound, and I suddenly heard a tone I wasn't used to from him. A sincere, sympathetic tone, as if he was about to really lay something on me that not even he wanted to say. He carried on and I descended further and now found myself realizing the true gravity of this situation I had gotten myself into.

CHAPTER 24

"There have been numerous reported complaints of persons expressing their dissatisfaction with you and the poor quality that your work has been reduced to. I'm in a compromising position, as you know, it reflects badly on me. How can you expect employees to respect me and follow rules and procedures while you make every effort to bend every rule possible? Young man, I wish I had opportunities you have at your disposal. You know how many people would like to be in your shoes? Think about it. One day you will regret you ever made things reach this far. You have been reporting to work at your convenience for the past 3 months. Your reports are not being submitted, the systems are failing. You just can't seem to handle your responsibilities. I'm sorry," he said my name then paused. "I'm sorry, but I have no choice than to let you go."

At that instant I felt a cold chill crawl up my spine and I went blank. I swore I would pass out. I remained silent, swallowing my sentence, as if a judge had just given me the death penalty. Keep calm, I thought to myself, this is your doing and this is not the time to create a scene. I might worsen things. Forget that, I instantly sprung into action.

I was now all too tired of the same old story, waking up looking forward to the usual awkward bumps along the corridor, the forged smiles. Everyone wants your attention, to complete something, or to do something. You escaping, and around the corner another waiting to collar you. In the presence of either a person, an attractive female that happens to steal all the stares for that brief time she's hired. Imagining yourself having the most sensual time in spaces; or on late submission of those reports that had to be on your boss's desk that week and you ain't even save the file, let alone type those first key strokes in Microsoft Word. Nerd surfing all day the three w's, on some imaginary highway where binary spinals, traffic roads of copper, they ride in all frequencies, all spectrums. If don't believe me just ask the geo-orbiting satellite above where a particular packet came from. The odds are astronomical but it is likely that I will give a yes node. Bored, never, as Facebook is my binoculars and YouTube house my friends, fun never ceases for at least after you spend all that time shoveling through all that junk or all what that tickle your fancies and you finally stumble onto something worthy of your boss's time. Before you know it you load up the video, minimize the page and decrease the volume; all in a one motion that would confuse you for some orchestra coordinator.

Everything suddenly sank in, the damage has been done, I got what I deserved, I thought. Mummy will catch a fit when she finds out. And to think all this time I put into this place, all for nothing. Look at me now. I stood up in the rage like a furious lion let out his cage.

Leaving now might preserve my sanity. Why am I even here wasting away in this claustrophobic space still?

"Y'all dun take everything from me, but no more!" I felt a sudden charge as blood rushed through my veins. "I must not waste a second here anymore. It's true that you fired me, fired me from an eternal sleep and I thank you for firing me, now I am awake and alive. You took everything from me the first time I came into this joint. You dun?? take away my voice, my sense of direction, my instinct and for what, a few pieces of silver with the queen's face and hand me down paper currency. I carried my cross and now, if you don't mind, I would like to bask in my thoughts that were once lost." And with a deep breath, I paused.

"Just great! You finally got what you wanted, right? I don't need you or this place. You have any idea what I've been going through lately? Do you? Wait, don't even answer, I've had just about enough of your condescending talk for a lifetime. And to think I used to want to be just like you. Thank you for opening my eyes. Forget you and your firm, you serving their interest alright, only concerned with the bottom line. What do you think, persons come to work here because they like to? Nah, never that, it's always been a means to an end. You conveniently forgot about all the late hours I put into this place, working on these systems, building the customer database and hand crafting reports. All to make y'all work easier. Installing all these hardware and running cables with no overtime. People look at me with envy but they don't know the half of it. How far you think that salary taking me?

You think you doing me a favor. All you'll do is drain us young people and dispose of us under the guise of underperformance, like slaves!"

"Are you finished?" he replied.

"It's sad, because sometimes I wish I never knew you. You have taken enough from me; you do not owe me anything. I accept your decisions and I'm a man that's free from these confines now. I have things I must do. As God is my witness, I will pull through."

Without hesitation I left his office calmly and proceeded to my department where I parked my stuff hurriedly in a garbage bag. And with a deep breath of exaltation, I gathered all energy left, tossing the garbage bag over my shoulder and without bidding anyone farewell I was out.

CHAPTER 25

"Hello!" I answered, annoyed and harsh. "Hello!" I said again.

A soft voice replied my name with a long pause.

"Yes?" I couldn't control my tone at this point. So much anger floating around in my head. I couldn't stomach any games at this point, anything that would subtract from my current disposition. She said my name again, this time softer and sweeter, as if sensing my mood and trying to sweeten things.

She returned with, "Baby, is something wrong? I've been calling and texting from yesterday with no reply. Is everything okay?"

"Not now Shari, my head hurts."

"Are you feeling alright?"

"I said my head hurts, why you asking me this stupid question?"

"I was just trying to…"

"You were trying to what? What can you possibly do to aid me right now?"

"Oh I'm sorry. You sound pissed. You wanna tell me bout it?"

I didn't respond. I was somewhere else right now. I should have never answered the phone. I should've let it just vibrate. I remained mute, taking a few deep breaths into the receiver.

"Not right now, Shari."

"Not right now! You have me worried sick. You mean you couldn't find the decency to answer a text or even respond to a call? Here I am at crunch time, minutes from my final exams, I calling your ass and you still can't find the decency at this point to respond. HELLO!"

I was lost in thought, I had totally forgotten about her finals and it's not like I intentionally blotted her out as if it's been all an easy stroll for me these days. I know she'll do well. Oh, well.

"Fine, just fine. I been meaning to talk to you. You have just been so distant lately; you haven't given me a chance to—"

She carried on, her voice was soughing, but I couldn't let it melt me, I couldn't let these feelings just disintegrate and die. No.

"Baby, I'm so nervous."

I finally gave in, "What do you want to talk to me about? Right now I have a laundry basket filled with problems I have no answers for. What can you possibly do to help me? What can you possibly do besides lending me your ears?"

"Choops."

"Shari right now is not the right time for this."

"But baby, I need to talk to you." she said it like she wanted to cry.

"Why? Why?" I returned angrily.

I stood at the door way outside the office with my garbage bag parcel on the clay brick foot path. A scene was erupting as if I could feel a hundred eyes from behind the tinted glass piercing me; probably they were wondering who I'm getting on so hysterical with on the other end of the line. I couldn't care less at this point; my mind was just bent on hitting something, anything that would render me numb.

"Why you always make things seem so poignant and they turn out to be nothing? I swear, you have this attention craze, girl. Behave. I'll call you later."

I hung up. I picked up the garbage bag and proceeded to walk to the bus stop. I couldn't articulate this rage. I felt like I had been used and left out in the cold. At this point I was impermeable to pain; I tossed the garbage bag over my shoulders and felt blood rushing to my head. Suddenly, I felt a tremor in my pocket then an eruption that would irritate me and push me beyond the tipping point. Although irritated I couldn't help but answer. I couldn't resist the urge; I had to express my frustration. I had to vent.

I answered with, "What is it now? Didn't I tell you we'll talk later?"

"It's important," she returned softly, waiting, almost looking for an invitation.

I sighed in annoyance and remained mute. I watched vehicles speed up and down passing me on the highway. My tie was blown to my back. All these motorists seemed to be in a mad rush today, probably late for something; an appointment or lunch date.

I said, "What is it?"

I heard a soft cry. Well, symptoms of a soft cry. She breathed heavily on the other end. Singing sorrow, soft sorrow as if she was in some pain, and then in a tearful voice she began again.

"You don't care, do you?"
"What has gotten into you?"

I could barely make out what she said. I proceeded to go and sit at the bus terminal away from the noise of the jet powered vehicles, placing my belongings in-between my legs.

She continued to rant. I was sympathetic to her pain and thinking I haven't been there for her lately. I know I haven't been as supportive as I ought to. How could I? I have all this shit dealing with at present. How could she possibly know? I don't want to burden her with my troubles at this point. She's worked so hard to get where she is. I don't want anything,

anything I bring to stand in the way of her dreams. She's almost there, I can feel the warmth in her tears, they hit my soul like sentimental rain drops, precipitating from the heavens, making everything anew with their blessings. I still love her like no other and it's truly killing me that her Paps been giving her hell lately. Could it be because of me?

She continued, "I realize you say less and less to me."
"Baby, what have I done? You know I going through a rough time. Just last night I got into it with my father again. I cried myself to sleep last night. Where were you when I needed you? Why weren't you answering your phone last night?"

I could tell she wasn't faking. She obviously wanted to share her pain with me but at this point, I couldn't bear any extra load.

"Baby", then she said my name. "What is wrong with you?"
"Where are you now?" she enquired.

I didn't answer.

"It doesn't sound like you in the office", she said inquisitively.
"Why aren't you at work?"
"I'm at school, in the back of the cafeteria taking some air. I wish I could do the presentation some other time. I feel like shit."

Oh yes, I remember now. She's been prepping so hard, on account of her practical exams which comes in the form of a debate or presentation. I think. She had to state her case and attempt to defend her client who was a hypothetical pharmaceutical company. I can't recall the minor details but I remember her saying it was worth 40% of her final grade. Law school, Hugh Wooding Law School to be precise. I could imagine her now, without all the crying and melodrama. I guess she is dressed in one of those black skirt suits she likes so much, looking oh so sophisticated and sexy. I remember seeing those suits hug her curves, cocoa-butter, soft ebony toned like dark gold melanin absorbing all the rays which shone. My Nafadit, my queen Nubian, my Delilah and my Sheba, my Caribbean diva, gift from the master architect. More than versatile, intellectually astute with a strut that would drive the most composed of men wild. I bet she has on the lip gloss she likes so much, that make her full lips even more inviting with her blush on each cheek adding dimension to her deep worm hole dimples, no pimples, off the rector, no scales could weigh, no seismologist could measure her impact on me.

She was much more than a pretty fac. You see, she was my friend way before the intimacy, and we connected and built private bridges to each other's hearts. I've always been lucky with the ladies and she was more than just a lady, she was a gem with hints of divinity. Forgive me for being blasphemous but we worshipped each other, selfishly. I never could have fathomed feeling this way about any other, well, except mother. Her long natty dreads, neatly tied in a ponytail keeping the freak restrained while in the studious school environment.

I can envision legal lingo leaving her lips, slowly painting them pretty with her trini-accent, despite their obscure and cumbersome pronunciations. I could see her standing in-front of the panel of examiners stating her case with the poise of a pro. She had a way with words and was the catalyst that sparked my interest in the *sublime and beautiful*.

"I have about 40 minutes before legal discourse. I have…"

"Oh lord! What is it with you, girl? You should be getting ready."

"I have to get something off my chest, baby"

"What is it? Is it another man? Have you met someone already?" I went on in a rage; I was compelled to have it out with her even though I myself must admit that I haven't been exactly faithful. Well, I had been, until last night; it wasn't premeditated and I was under the influence and all. She must have met the guy a while now. She wouldn't just give herself up - I know her.

"I knew it! I knew you couldn't be trusted. I had a feeling this would come. My boys warned me about this."

"Met someone!" she answered in surprise.

"Listen," she shouted and said my name sternly; this time her sweetness was gone. "I'm …I'm pregnant."

"You what!" I responded like a reflex.

"I didn't stutter, I said I'm pregnant! I'm carrying your baby. That's what I've been trying to tell you. Baby! Hello! Baby this is not the time to get cold on me."

At this point, I was feeling a million sensations, like I had landed in a red ant nest and with the inhabitants stinging me on every inch of my anatomy. Is this fo'real? I'm awake? I can't be. But I am and everything came tumbling down.

"That's what I've been trying to tell you, baby. That's why I've been having these arguments with my father lately. I've known for 3 weeks now, I took about 3 tests, all dem say de same thing. Baby I'm anxious, I'm scared, I don't want to lose you, I don't know what to do."

I had to step in and be a man at this point. "Baby, relax, everything's gonna be okay, relax get ready for your finals, I'll call you later, I just have something I need to deal with. I'll call you. I promise. Good luck.

"Baby before you make another untimely exit, one of my friends was telling me something about you this morning. Is everything alright? Is it true? Rochell told me last night at the club you were getting all touchy feely with Keisha and y'all left together."

As if things could get worse. I remained composed and answered, "I'll call you later, Babes. I have to go now. Bye."

CHAPTER 26

I might as well wave my entire future plans goodbye at this point. Damn, all of a sudden everything comes toppling down. I swear these past few months I've seen more dramatic scenarios than I can expose at present; it bewilders me to the point of insanity. Out of nowhere everything just changed. It's odd, it's like my life has been derailed and I'm on my final destination. Either something is going to happen to me or I'm being shaped into something else. Whatever it is I can sense a lot of anger and hostility growing inside of me. Will I fall victim to these emotions and be another statistic or can I rise above it? Right now I wouldn't be surprised whatever the future brings. All this time success still manages to elude me, I have managed to descend rather than climb. Why do I feel so low?

I went home to drop off my stuff. I stumbled on a picture of my grandparents looking happy and free as two brown doves in a tree. I thought to myself, why are they so happy? I'll tell you the truth. I have never seen a pair happier and to think they were farmers toiling under the hot sun in bananas, day by day for a living. My granddad in the pic sported one of them those old farmer overalls and this cowboy hat, his cutlass in one hand and piece of bamboo in the other. Granny right next, sporting her usual smile, getting a little shade under the banana leaves, while he seemed to prop up one of these banana trees with the bamboo. Working always seemed more therapeutic to them and less about the ends. I always wondered why they worked so hard. In those times farming was the lifeblood of our country; their success came from toiling under the sun. That didn't deter them one bit though. And they're still working so hard at their age. I found myself escaping the normal physical labour route and still success eludes me. What is success anyway and now that I'm unemployed, how do I attain that success I have been thirsting for so dearly? How can I achieve that state of mind they had? I'm still bent on getting fired but life goes on. I think of myself as talented and well qualified so I better start using my skills set to do something positive. Something I can look forward to, waking up to. It's going to be hard but God got me this far for a reason.

What equates success?

Opportunity bewildered me to the point of paranoia. Ideas like tears sometimes spontaneously appear, trickle down, then disappear without a trace. Sparks ignite the mind to concepts lost in that short space of time between those moments you own it and search for your notepad to ink it in. Doesn't quite materialize as thought; let's step back to examine the thought, for sport. How can you scrutinize every eureka moment you have and how do you assess its worthiness? Stuffed in that back closet in your mind is where you find ideas one of a kind, stacked like boxes, infested with webs of deceased spiders. Everything somehow withers away but that idea closet remains.

Today's commercial-driven arena redefines success. Packaged and processed in an attractive display is one of this place's greatest illusions. The master manipulator of it all is He, without losing focus on the task I reserve the right to leave *him* a mystery. Reconsider this sentence. Thinking about the new saying should be *"money maketh man."* Son, soon you will understand that you may not be defined by what's in your brain; rather, what's in your hand. Grasping this concept might prove easier for the now generation who live, eat and sleep in this fabricated existence fueled by money. Funny, ain't it, just a couple years ago I was taught money is the root of all evil and now I am taught that's all I need to know. Kartel said it best: *"money is the universal grammar."* So does that universal grammar equate success?

The answer is yes and no.

Success I see as a continuous process, like aging, you continue to succeed as time progresses and as you excel in your craft. The acclaim that follows is just a mere byproduct of success. You are successful when you have transcended, when you are no longer at the beginners' level. It's now to your back. Successful is a handful and can only mean that you have succeeded success and now into that realm of recurring successes.

The price to pay for success is hidden under the mascara of the successor. As I look with dismay it's sad to say that the popular opinion sways what we know today as success. Everyone loves it when your work gets recognition. You feel good, don't you? Better yet when you get compensated for it. Reward fuels you to do more, work harder, let flow more of these creative juices that you left fermenting all these years. Consumed by this instant gratification notion stationed in the backroom, craving the spotlight. Everyone, come look at me - 'I'm special'.

CHAPTER 27

There are times in one's life when the quest takes over and starts becoming the sole purpose of one's existence. Questioning everything in my circumference in order to understand my purpose in this place, my role in life's theatre. Time lay as a journal. Where must I go, what must I do; pursue or be pursued, succumb or overcome? Hailing from wherever I was conceived. I think I was conceived to unravel this elaborate puzzle. That's what I think, I don't know. I was given no manual, no tutorial along with this life, no guarantees I might get it right. Destiny bewilders me, dreams seem to be in my grasp but laugh when I try to feel them, live them. Words taught to me by those further down life's road paved my path. How do I know what's meant for me? How can I get a glimpse of destiny?

Caught somewhere between righteousness and prosperity, it's hard enough; I had enough; I can't attain any presently so I just lie there taking life as it is given to me.

My weakness is the flesh. I fantasize every time she walks by. Knowing that she belongs to someone else plays no part in the discussions undertaken. She is multiplied by the multitude I see; whether they are walking the streets, taking my order behind a counter, attending to a customer or laying there aimlessly awaiting life's end or steadily anticipating life's beginning. I feel like I haven't begun to live, my experiences a mere twinkle in the heavens, my actions revealing to onlookers what I've been hiding. Left to moan was a soul, left to wither in an abundance of food, concealed by my confines, by this 8 by 10 box, from where all imagination is stifled. It's strange but deep inside yourself, you already have the answer, although (you) knowing how to alter fate, you sit still and wait. Waiting for life's fuel, the fuel which sustains motivation and catapults you to the summit, where all the like minds dwell. In this place the auras of running mates baffle the onlookers; the thirst is not bad enough. Out of the billions out there, you're pursuing relentlessly what makes you different. The architect managed to make you unique but you're still just like all of them; working, trying, aspiring for the better. At twenty three, I have learnt nothing that could entitle me to be mentioned in the same breath as all of them, they who battle every opponent, every obstacle hindering the light. That minute light escaping under these doors drew me. Praying might exhale blessings daily but still will not suffice. Life drove me lazy, trying to retrace times when the fire led me up all night, not dreaming but living. I remember walking the streets at three in the morning, not a soul in sight, unafraid despite my baggage, my laptop wrapped snug in my weathered Jansport backpack. Disguised as a hoodlum steadily pacing, praying, I reach my apartment safe, trying the unknown streets of Curepe as I trod from the university to my cardboard apartment. What possessed me then?

What held me together in those times is now lost, submerged under everything life threw. I wonder …can I still resurrect what was lost?

It doesn't matter what goes on internally, whatever fantasies forged in memory may not translate to reality. Others may never recognize your imprint because it remains captive by fear. How hard can it be to express all these suppressed feelings locked away? The contents of greatness live in showmanship. Of course hard work bears little recognition when you slave in the dark. I have to get out the dark, I have to get out…Where is that spark?

Forces hidden deep down propel me to be great. I feel it ever so often as my blood heats up from this passion.

A talented son, mom's oldest son, pap's only one, destined to reach the sun. Let it be known through the alleys of the city. Let my name moan through the valleys, bearing witness to my finest. Yes, I am he, stated like a dreamer of the highest caliber, as the water drenched my nappy hair; I swear I can taste the dream. Coldest in the morning, shocking when it hits, yet the wetness couldn't subdue the dream in my eyes. They say the therapy of a bath washes everything away, refreshing you for the new day. As heavy as my head is, I still feel there is room up there to be filled.

Chapter 28

I suddenly felt fearless, like I can take on the world head on even if things looked bleakest for me now with no job and on top of this unexpected news from Shari. Well at least I have some money saved up and mom still has her little hairdressing going on; we will manage. And oh how can I forget my little scene with the fellas. Later will be greater, no backing out now. I won't even burden anyone with the news of my unemployment or Shari's pregnancy just yet. I have to give her a call; I don't even know how we will deal with that. I know that was the last thing either of us was expecting, so what will become of this scenario? At present I really don't know.

A little thrill is all I can ask for at this time; anything, matters not, minute or grand. And grand it will be. So crazy, the plan rolled out my tongue while asleep. Anticipating the call of the wild, my blood seems to draw me near as I am overwhelmed by this feeling, not fear but a chill that itches down to the marrow.

After speaking to Shari I was blank; without a dream to carry me through the night. The dark night erased everything in sight as I felt for the first time fear, that uncertain chill running down your spine. As it came to pass, I was alone, alone with my thoughts, no wind to whisper company. Only the dead of night piercing my sides, oozing out truths, (though) loud with truths that only I was privy to.

CHAPTER 29

Everything was all black—black denim, black boots, black stockings masking, fastening my identity under the negligee stocking, wearing the stench of stale funk. State of mind— blank, as we trace lines to our fate. Wait, heavy; armed with a cutlass—but for this occasion call it a machete— steady the scene unfolding as my eyes escape and gleamed?? for the reaps of our pillage. The stage is set as we began our descent. We knew that building all too well and for whatever reason this building stood for, it was weaved in each of our fabrics and it had played some important roles in our development, our shape. I hope that the unraveling fate is for the best, besides, it's a sure thing, right….no security, easy access. Bless Simon to come up with this idea. Lord knows I wouldn't have stumbled upon it even if it stood naked, wrapped in a big red bow written 'take me' across. I would toss too much at nights if I hadn't explored the possibilities or might I say the benefits of this little job. Oh it's a job alright. I work so I have to be compensated, even if that compensation is theirs. The monies that they stole from the man they sold their ticket - sold him hope. I bet you that man playing lotto for years. Look at him, walking stick not even holding steady, appearing to be under the influence. My influence at this present time is the present and the void it will fill once this hit is fulfilled. I'll take mine in cash. Cold, as I froze for a minute to summarize all that was going on inside me and around me. Selling dreams to chasers, hoping that luck, their luck, might strike the jackpot.

We all got into the rental, a beat-up red jeep, windows inky black, coated with a red paint that looked devilish under the surrounding darkness. We all got in and in an instant we sped off. No music, just the three of us in the dark seeing stars on the dashboard, light entering through the windscreen as we entered the highway, praying to God we don't fall victim to a random highway search. Simon our handyman on the wheels at the wheel knew his way around vehicles from a tyke, inside and underneath them. Dressed in oil-stained shorts and vest, still every afternoon after school he joined us on the court for the random game of 21. Those were the only times my cousin and I really built together. The two of us both being raised simultaneously on the opposite ends of the family. His mom, my aunt on my father's side and a more shady and comfortable side it was. Simon always knew what he wanted to do and after form 5 he did just that. He began working with his father at his garage and became a ghost after. No one saw him hanging around.

Danny was in the back on the passenger side; mute, assuming his regular state, as if lost in some orgy of thoughts infesting his mind. Danny wore anything, meaning he was down for anything, the hothead; never get him red because I assure you that you would live to regret it. after. Danny was not like us; he was more seasoned and had been involved in a lot of different things since we left secondary school. A lot of different hits – didn't matter, big hit, small hit, extortion, armed robbery. He was the first man to show me a gun, I felt its cold surface, I held it and felt the rush that so many my age feel when they grip the steel, almost fitting perfect in my arms as I held it steady, aiming the machine at the air. Aimless, yet the power of the weapon almost makes you envision a target in front of you and the fear it aroused in your target. I knew why Simon brought Danny along and that scared me and I also knew he almost always had his piece with him.

Danny changed, like we all did but his change far exceeded ours. It seemed like he was always a big man handling big money, doing big things way before we had such in our reach. He hung with one of our flashiest drug runners named Chico. They call him that because he has a white pit named Chico. Everybody say they look alike. Man and dog almost inseparable. His yellow Latino complexion along with the pit bull's all white shining coat make them both stand out even before the fact of his profession got your attention. He was very resourceful in our city and to both sides of the field, the police and the criminals using him to their advantage. Danny was one of the young boys he put under his wing. Obviously he saw potential in him and saw that he could come in very handy. Danny and I skipped class regularly to run the streets, chasing anything that caught our interest for the day. We chased skirts many times around town and for a while I thought of myself as a track star running all around the place. We chased arcades, we chased money, opportunity, any little thing that would get us at least five dollars. Those 5 dollars of course we would use to buy long loaves called sixties, costing 60 cents apiece, cheese and soft drinks and sometimes we'd just idle away at the Derek Walcott Square.

I wiped my face with my rag, cold sweat trickled down the back of my neck and seemed to settle on my back leaving a cold feeling settling inside as I render myself numb to whatever was going to take place. I was there for one reason and it didn't involve either me playing a good mediator if we happened to be pulled over or my ability to quiet any hint of mischief. No, I had a far greater purpose and ensured that everything went undetected and assured its covert title. I for one wouldn't have taken up this without thinking and playing out every possible scenario. And every feature my mind fabricated would have been for more confirmation, strengthening the chances of success.

CHAPTER 30

I felt a tug and suddenly my phone beeped and a text came through. Shari had sent a text telling me "Everything's going to be alright baby. Just hold on cause things are going to be fine with us. Something special is growing inside me, I know it's too soon but I can feel it - something beautiful. No regrets, no fears, no worries honey – it's we us against the world."

"What am I thinking! What I'm I thinking! Fellas! Fellas, wait!" I yelled.

I should stop this before I do something I might regret for the rest of my life. I don't want to end up regretting, ending up like so many of my friends have. I shouldn't resort to this. There has to be a better way, there has to be a better way to solve my problems.

"Stop!" I yelled at Simon. "Stop Now!"

"What's going on?" returned Simon

"I said stop now."
He pulled over the highway.
"Do you know what we are about to do, fellas?" I said sternly. "Have we really thought this thing through?" Simon returned.

"But we spoke bout this already, everything is accounted for. Relax, everything will be fine. In and out, remember," confirmed Simon.

"What was in these boxes would see us $30,000 up. We would separate it evenly and build a studio like we always spoke about," he said, his words enticing me to cave in. But at that moment I realized what was really important, nothing is was going to make me succumb, like so many of my brothers.

I opened the door and jumped out.

"Wait, how can you just leave us like that?" he yelled from the window.

I didn't answer; I placed my hood over my head and started walking away.

"You know we can't do this without you, you know that," he continued, bringing the vehicle to a halt.

I turned and said, "Well don't, then. Can't you see this goes against everything we stood for? Simon, how can you have come this far?"

I looked him dead in the eye, looking for the friend I knew but he was gone. His eyes seemed so dark. Before he could even reply, Danny jumped in.

"We don't need you dread, you wasting our time. You see, Simon? I told you he would just complicate things. Think about it, more money for us. You pussy boy, you see why we don't lime no more, cause you have no fucking balls. De only reason why you here is because you have that door alarm scrambler."

"Well, is that so, pardner? Here!" I tossed it to him. I couldn't care less at this point. "Here, now you ain't need me again."

I had a door alarm scrambler from last summer while I interned at this security firm. I think it works by doing a sort of brute force dictionary attack on the alarm system, disabling the audible alarm while using various combinations of the fail-safe security codes that manufactures put in it. Anyhow I wrote a bunch of code and put it into machine language with a compiler then loaded it onto an SD card onto the scrambler. My added code made the scrambler interface with that particular alarm. All that had to be done was to attach the scrambler using the IEEE port to the back of the terminal at the door. Simon had seen me do it before so he shouldn't have any problems, I thought to myself

"I can't do this, not now, not ever, it's too much." I said.

"Fine, suit yourself. Don't want you here when we collect all of the money from the content in those boxes, though. I can't believe you, man. Some friend you are. Let's go, Simon!" replied Danny.

I saw Simon that night for the last time. I can still remember that look he gave me as they moved off like they were going away somewhere for a long time. Like it was ordained and they couldn't resist the pull.

CHAPTER 31

It all really causes one to think critically about the nature of this here system, and its numerous flaws in design. Are they flaws? Everything is by intelligent design. Trying to come to turns with the mentality that results in our young soldiers becoming causalities, victims of their over-compensated feelings. Feelings of desperation. It takes time to develop and there are numerous variables which contribute to that despair but it all eventually spills into more killing, when things reach its breaking point. From whatever angle you view the recent chain of events, one thing is evident. Why does it feel like we are left few alternatives to resort to? We have a serious a problem there. Why are so many of us venting and resorting to crime? I'm sure the answers are all hidden in plain sight, you just have to know where to look. Who really wants answers these days anyway, it's hard enough just surviving.

We're all hurdling full-speed towards death with no awareness of our own extinction.

Every time a person close to us dies a part of us leaves with them, our souls are forever stained, never the same, the life is one hell of a ride where your destination might just be over the curb. Our choices greatly influence the duration of our lives to some extent. Was he predestined to go so soon? Are we driven to death prematurely because of our predispositions? Who knows, it may all be rigged. This place ain't a joke, you can't let the game get to your head. You cannot let the pursuits of desire and wants cloud your vision and have you doing things you may never come back from. Something random like a passing police vehicle happened to intrude on the whole scene going down. And instead of them surrendering they engaged fire. POW!!

Danny was lucky to have minor injuries. Simon on the other hand wasn't so fortunate. I could easily have been in his place. And to think that it was all cool just a week ago. That's why I say this place resembles hell. A plantation in hell, where you either serve the masters of the day or die chasing freedom. He died chasing the rewards we thought would come out of that robbery. He thought it would help him to have financial freedom. I'm saddened by the loss and I will never be the same but he's free now. Free from this damn place.

CHAPTER 32

I've grown too accustomed to this, this meager kind of living. I wonder if my peers have such potent thoughts as mine or even share my sentiments. I've realized that I live in a society that's a mirror of the previous slave plantation we're supposedly emancipated from. Gone are the days when we were considered chattel, the machine has become more covert in disguising their mastery of our psyches but I see it and you see it too. Its evidence is everywhere and its effects touch everyone of us in some way or another. As we sit in our cozy abodes glued to our screens, we lose sight of what's happening, we drift into this fabricated existence fed to us by the very people who swore years ago their superiority and who have gone to great heights to maintain their vice grip hold. Listen, I'm far from a liberator, I'm not a freedom fighter, not a historian, or a public intellectual; no—I'm disenfranchised, I refuse to follow orders and I insist on challenging the status quo. I cannot be labeled because I refuse to be limited by your shallow assumptions, like those of our previous colonialists did in their attempt at making us seem inferior.

The office and the plantation are no different. They both operate with the intent of generating profits, they both have hierarchies of leadership and dominance and they both go through great lengths to ensure that the psyche of the labourers are moulded to prevent resistance and maintain compliance. They both exploit those at the bottom of the hierarchy and keep them under an inferiority complex. I hate this concept; I love commerce and believe in business and enterprise. I also understand that every position in an organisation, however mundane, contributes to the ultimate goal of the organisation and towards the final products. What I don't understand is the exploitation, the greed and the conflict that arises from what is (a) foremost a cooperative effort to begin with. I apologize if I'm a little old-fashioned or a virgin in matters of the world. All I know is that I see their lies and deceit and most of you do too! All I know is that this will continue unless we exercise our freedoms, build our own empires and run this shit ourselves.

So far are we now, from what was considered the most horrific crime of humanity, a crime of a nation. Like hardware we were auctioned on their blocks, like cattle we were reared on their plantations. Stripped away from our identity, forgotten was our culture, our way of life. We are very fortunate to come from such a strong race. We've been through it all and still go through, yet we survive. Through their efforts, destinies changed; they fought for our rights, for our future, so those that would emerge after can have it better. I know I have that same fight in me, somewhere deep it lies untapped—the spirit that is the driving force toward dreams and aspirations! The road is narrow and the journey long but my people keep moving with rhythm and style, so that old Negro spiritual can never die. As we move forward, we grow, we mature, and the value of knowledge, of self, is penniless in this penny-run world. My people, lift your heads up high. My people, stretch and reach for the sky. The struggle is overshadowed by the reward, so don't cry.

EPILOGUE

Excerpt from "The Over-Soul", by *Ralph Waldo Emerson.*

If we consider what happens in conversation, in reveries, in remorse, in times of passion, in surprises, in the instructions of dreams, wherein often we see ourselves in masquerades, - the droll disguises only magnifying and enchanting a real element, forcing it our distinct notice, - we shall catch many mints that will broaden and lighten into knowledge of the secrets of nature. All goes to show that the soul in man is not an organ, but animates and exercises all the organs; is not a function, like the power of memory, of calculation, of comparison, but uses these as hands and feet; is not a faculty, but a light; is not the intellect or the will, but the mastering of the intellect and the will; is the background of our being, in which they lie, - an immensity not possessed and that cannot be possessed. From within or from behind, a light shines through us upon things, and makes us aware that we are nothing, but the light is all. A man is a façade of a temple wherein all wisdom and all good abide. What we commonly call man, the eating, drinking, planting, counting man, does not as we know him, represent him, but misrepresents him. Him we do not respect, but his soul, whose organ he is, would he let it appear through his actions, would make our knees bend, when it breathes through his intellect, it is genius; when it breathes through his will, it is virtue; when it flows through his affection, it is love. And the blindness of the intellect begins, when it would be something of itself. The weakness of the will begins, when the individual would be something of himself. All reforms aim, in some one particular, to let the soul have its way through us; in other words, to engage us to obey.

Ralph Waldo Emerson, *The Over-Soul*, (1841)

Special Thanks To

-Cassia Joseph

-The Ministry of Tourism, Heritage and

Creative Industries

-Dr. Kentry Jn. Pierre

-Allan Weekes

-Celina Jean & Joseph Grames Jean

-Kelvin B. Jean

-Rosalia Langellier

And all those who encouraged me along the process.